SPLIT IMAGE

Also by Ron Faust from Tom Doherty Associates

The Burning Sky
Fugitive Moon
In the Forest of the Night
Lord of the Dark Lake
When She Was Bad

RON FAUST

SPLIT IMAGE

A TOM DOHERTY ASSOCIATES BOOK
NEW YORK

This is a work of fiction. All of the characters and events portrayed in this novel are either fictitious or are used fictitiously.

SPLIT IMAGE

This book is printed on acid-free paper.

A Forge Book
Published by Tom Doherty Associates, Inc.
175 Fifth Avenue
New York, NY 10010

Forge® is a registered trademark of Tom Doherty Associates, Inc.

Library of Congress Cataloging-in-Publication Data

Faust, Ron.
Split image / Ron Faust.—1st ed.
p. cm.
"A Forge book"—T.p. verso.
ISBN 0-312-86011-0
I. Title.
PS3556.A98S66 1997
813'.54—DC21 96-54156
CIP

First Edition: June 1997

Printed in the United States of America

0 9 8 7 6 5 4 3 2 1

. . . the theory of a new birth and the remission of sins through the shedding of blood have all their origins in savagery . . .

—Sir James Frazer
The Golden Bough

PART I

Crows

ONE

The rift in the fog closed before I could notch an arrow. Visibility was only about twenty yards. A few yards beyond that limit the buck waited, his ears erect, his moist nostrils flexing as he tasted the air. I was downwind; I had made no sound, had not moved, and yet he sensed my presence, the danger, death. He had eluded death for many seasons: his size and the spread of his antlers told me that. He was old, a patriarch of the Cervidae.

The damp fog chilled my sweat. Snowflakes fluttered like moths through the mist. Fog had bleached color from the October woods, the russets and browns and pale golds and the scarlet pennants of Virginia creeper. The birch trees were luminous.

We, the deer and I, patiently waited together in a diminished and distorted arena. We were enemies and complicitors.

We stood less than thirty yards apart on an old dirt logging road that hadn't been used in years. There was a drainage ditch on either side of the weedy tire ruts, and then the land rose, gently at first, then more steeply into the round glacier-carved hills.

Currents of air played sly tricks with the fog. Forms assembled and dissolved like hallucinations.

The buck defecated. I could smell it.

I notched an arrow and slowly drew it back. The string bit into my index and middle fingers. I had no calluses there; I was not an archer, not a hunter, really. But the sudden emergence of the deer had excited in me a sickly greed.

The fog swirled, thinned; I saw the buck; he vanished and soon after reappeared. Perspective was falsified in this light; it was difficult to estimate the size or distance of an object and its exact relation to other objects. The buck was staring toward me. His eyes were big, disproportionate to the delicacy of his head, and they gleamed black and moist.

I did not consciously aim. I didn't deliberately release the arrow. There was the soft twang of bowstring and a thin, bright shaft of light that linked my hand to the deer's flesh. (*Flèche,* I remembered thinking earlier, was French for "arrow.") The deer seemed catapulted into the air. He landed stiff-legged, ran a few yards before falling, quickly rose, and as he bounded off into the mist I saw the white flag of his tail.

Beginner's luck, I thought. It was almost as if the deer had willed the arrow into his body. I felt no pity. That surprised me—the lack of pity.

I advanced and saw the starbursts of blood staining the sodden autumn leaves. Bright red blood, oxygenated lung blood, confirmed what I had sensed: he was mortally wounded. My deer, my kill. I had not known that killing could provide such an explosive emotional relief.

It was snowing harder now. Snow was beginning to accumulate, dusting the ground and limning the black trees. I must find him before his tracks and blood trail were covered by snow. I could not lose him now. The act was not completed until I ritually cut his throat.

I stood in the cold and falling snow and textured fog, aware of the smells of wood rot and deer feces. Far off in the mist some crows cawed. Maybe they were observing the flight of my deer. Snowflakes ticked softly as they landed. For a moment I considered retreating to the cabin. This was a mystical foolishness—there was not a life to be discovered in death.

The splashes of blood led across the drainage ditch and up an embankment to a clearing and then up a ravine between steep hills. Smooth oval stones lay in the ravine, and bare white sticks of wood like driftwood, like bones, were scattered around. You could see that the ravine was the bed of a creek during the spring thaw, a torrent then, with rapids and falls and, on the level stretches, clear, rippling pools. But now only mist flowed down the ravine, obeying the contours of land, pouring down the dry streambed with a ghastly silence. The deer bled profusely as he climbed. The streaks and splashes and dribbles of blood were like a strange alphabet on the clean white snow. I paused to dip a finger in the blood and taste it—salty and sweet, and beginning to congeal now.

The hills rose steeply on both sides. Here there were pine and fir trees scattered among the oaks and maples and birch, clawed brush, and bare tangled vines of wild grape and blueberry. The outraged cawing of the crows sounded closer now.

The fog thinned as I climbed, and finally I reached a ridge and could see clearly down into a small meadow cupped in the hills. The mist there lay in isolated pools and tatters that writhed in the faint breeze. Snow was falling thickly now, turning the ground white.

I halted. I was winded. My legs trembled. I was weak from my excitement and exertion.

Below, at the far end of the hollow, a man kneeled by a fallen deer—my deer. His bare arms were bloody to the elbows. Half a dozen crows, as black and glossy as obsidian, were perched high in a bare oak. They harshly denounced the man and the deer and me. Hateful crows, a demonic chorus. I almost turned back because of the crows.

I tacked down the steep hill, digging in my heels, clambered over a fallen birch whose papery skin had been shredded by bears' claws, crossed the level ground, and had almost reached the man when he sensed my presence. He turned quickly but did not rise. He gripped a knife in his left hand. The sleeves of his wool flannel shirt had been rolled to the biceps, and his forearms were bloody. The deer's viscera were spilled out onto the snow, dark red organs and loose slimy coils of intestine that steamed in the cold. There was a bitter metallic odor. Open us up, I thought, and we stink like that. The soft glitter had gone out of the deer's eyes; now they were as lifeless as the glass eyes of a taxidermist's replica.

On his knees, his upper body half-turned, the man looked at me. After a moment he inclined his head in a brief nod. His eyes, behind aviator-style glasses, were amused.

"You surprised me," he said. "I almost cut off my thumb."

"That's my deer," I said.

"What?"

"That"—I pointed—"is my buck."

"No," he said. He smiled.

"This is my buck. I put an arrow in him down below. I tracked him here."

"No," he said, seeming both sympathetic and amused. "Sorry."

I could not judge his height, but he was about my age, early forties, wide across the shoulders, and his bloody forearms were thick-boned and well muscled. His hair was black. Straight black hair and black mustache and black eyebrows and lashes. His eyes were blue and his skin light, a sort of pale gold, flushed now with the cold. He had the eyes and complexion of a blond, but his hair was as black as the crows.

"You look cold," he said. "Want a drink?"

I shook my head.

He wore rubber-cleated hiking boots, jeans faded almost white, and a black- and gray-checked wool shirt. A dirty suede sheepskin-lined coat had been tossed aside. Leaning against the tree was a compound bow, an intricate device with a series of pulleys and balance weights and a sight. It was a machine. My borrowed bow, with which I'd shot the deer, was primitive in comparison.

He dropped the bloody knife and stood up. We were the same height.

"Are you sure you won't have a drink?"

I shrugged.

He lifted his bloody hands. "We'll shake another time."

"I don't know if we will."

"Does that mean you refuse to drink with me?" He wiped his hands on his jeans, removed a silver half-pint flask from a back pocket, and unscrewed the cap. "Brandy," he said. "Armagnac, actually. Good stuff. Here."

I hesitated for a moment (he noticed and was amused), then accepted the flask and took a swallow. "Thanks."

"Skoal," he said, and he drank deeply and returned the flask to his pocket.

"Skoal," I said, "means 'skull' in Danish."

"Does it now?"

"The Vikings used to drink out of human skulls."

"Did they? Leaky vessels, I would think. But then they didn't have Styrofoam."

He was confident and relaxed. He had that wry, tough, challenging style that you saw in young men who gather on street corners. There was something about me that seemed to amuse him, but he was not contemptuous.

"This is going to be a bitch of a storm," he said.

"Yes."

"I heard some crashing around in the brush toward the north. That way." He pointed. "Your deer, probably."

"No, this is my deer. This one. Your buck is crashing around in the brush over there—to the north."

He smiled. "I'm serious."

"So am I."

"Look, stand back a minute while I finish cleaning out this carcass, and then I'll help you track down your deer."

"This is my buck."

"But it isn't," he said. "I've told you that it isn't. You could choose to believe me. You *could* assume that I'm not a liar and a thief."

"You could assume the same of me."

"I do. It's just that you're mistaken."

"Stand aside," I said. "After I finish cleaning my deer I'll help you look for the other one, the one over there, to the north. Crashing around in the brush."

He laughed briefly, but there were now lines of tension around his eyes and mouth. "Slow down," he said. He stared levelly into my eyes. I was sorry that he was angry; I liked him, but I could not surrender on this small point of honor. The deer meant nothing to me—flesh I would not eat, a rack of antlers I would not have mounted, a near-accidental kill that might cause me shame tomorrow. Even so, I could not back down now.

Finally he said, "All right. I'll share the beast half and half with you."

"It's all mine."

"I'll give you this deer. A gift. I insist that you accept this buck as a present."

"You can't give me what is already mine."

"Take it."

"No," I said. "But I'll give it to you. This deer is now yours. I have given it to you."

"I refuse."

"I can't very well accept as a present what is already mine. But I can give away what is mine. Take the deer. It's yours now."

He laughed. "No, no. Here, we'll split the buck half and half. I give you my share as a gift; you give me your share."

I saw the absurdity of our quarrel as well as he, but I couldn't quit; I couldn't laugh. "But the deer is *all* yours now. I have given it to you."

"Thank you," he said, smiling. "And now I return it."

"I do not accept."

He stared at me, his shoulders hunched, perhaps thinking about hitting me, or perhaps trying to determine if I was joking. (I was joking, and I was not.)

"Oh, well, fuck you," he said, and he abruptly turned and kneeled by the deer. His hand reached into the snow for the bloody knife. I drew my own knife from its sheath.

I don't know how long I sat there after killing him. It was probably not more than ten or fifteen minutes. Snow dusted the deer. Snowflakes melted on the man's cheek and sparkled briefly in his hair. My mind was empty. I did not remember killing him. It had been like the deepest of sleeps. I returned to myself aware that the crows were still perched high in a nearby oak, still cawing crow obscenities.

What was the crow's-eye view of this bloody tableau? An eviscerated deer, a murdered man, blood everywhere, and me, as motionless as the dead.

It occurred to me—and this was my first conscious thought upon "awakening"—that the crows did not *object* to the carnage. Of course not. They were scavengers and were impatiently waiting their opportunity. Even so, I could not entirely dispel the notion that they were judging me—small black magistrates, feathery clerics.

He was lying prone on the snow. The knife was still in my hand. I was shocked by the savagery of my attack: the man had been stabbed and slashed and hacked—"butchered," the newspapers might say, "assaulted with a maniacal fury." I could not deny the truth of that. My blackout did not excuse me. There it was, and here I was, convicted in my own heart and mind, but still very calm and dreamy. I felt no guilt, no remorse. Only the crows had witnessed the murder.

I washed my hands with clean snow, removed the silver flask from the man's back pocket, and sipped the brandy. Skoal. Well, it was done, permanent, eternal. I could not expect to deal with the moral and philosophical aspects now. That might require the remaining years of my life. But at this moment I felt nothing. My act was without meaning, as incoherent and purposeless as a child's impulsive cruelty to a kitten.

I emptied the flask, wiped it clean, and dropped it into the snow. My knife went back into its sheath. Did I have everything? Each article of clothing, my wallet, wristwatch, the bow and quiver of arrows. Were any buttons missing from my coat? Hat, muffler. Wait—the arrow I had shot into the deer. I must retrieve that. I circled the dead man and saw that the shaft sticking out of the deer was milled aluminum with red vanes. The arrows in the man's quiver were aluminum with red vanes. Mine were old, of grainy wood, and the vanes were yellow. And now I saw that this deer was smaller than mine and his rack had fewer points. So then, my deer *had* run into the brushy country to the north, was probably still there, dead or dying.

It was only ten minutes to ten. Snow was still coming down hard and would last, covering my tracks, the deer, the dead man, the blood, my crime.

The filthy crows mocked me until I vanished from the clearing.

TWO

I returned the way I had come, across the little clearing, up the steep hill to a ridge, and then down the crooked ravine between thickly wooded hills to the logging road. The snow had covered my old footprints. Patches of fog remained in the low country.

I was about halfway back to the cabin when I heard a sound and halted. Men talking. There were other hunters in the woods: I'd heard voices early this morning, remote and muffled by fog, sourceless. Maybe the hunters ahead were friends of the dead man, his hunting partners. Maybe they were looking for him. I went on.

A few minutes later I walked around a bend and saw two men sitting on a log that lay tangentially to the trail. I stopped, forced myself to go on, stopped again.

"Morning," one of them said.

"Good morning."

They were big, overweight, red-faced men in middle age. One had not shaved for a week or so. They looked enough alike to be brothers. Both wore camouflage outfits and had their trousers tucked into their boots paratrooper-style.

"Looks like you had some luck," the bearded man said.

He was referring to the blood on my jacket and hands. "I helped my partner clean his deer," I said.

"Looks like you crawled into the cavity."

There was a liter bottle of bourbon set upright between them on the log. A compound bow was propped against a birch; a crossbow, with its wicked short bolt cocked in place, lay on the snow.

I nodded toward the crossbow. "Does that work pretty well?"

"Shit, I wouldn't know," the bearded man said. "Haven't seen a deer in three days, haven't seen a track, haven't imagined I seen a track."

"Haven't seen a woman," the other man said. "Haven't seen the spoor of a woman."

"Bow hunting stinks."

"First year we tried it."

"And the last year, too, Bo."

"Where are you guys from?" I asked.

"Milwaukee," the bearded man said. "Home of Sorenson Tool and Die. I'm Sorenson."

"I'm Tool and Die," the other man said. "You from around here?"

"Yes," I lied. "I've lived here all my life."

"Tough luck."

They laughed. They were drunk.

"You ever shoot a deer with that old bow of yours?" the bearded man asked.

"This bow? No."

"It looks like it might be the prototype, the original bow of bows."

"The bow lost in the mists of history," the other man said. "Adam's bow."

"Your partner use a bow like that?"

"No. He has a modern bow."

"Well, bud, it seems to me that if you're going to fail to shoot a deer, it's better to fail to shoot one with a cheap old bow like yours than to fail to shoot one with an expensive new bow like mine."

"Right," I said. "Nice talking to you. Good luck."

"We'll save your good luck for gun season," the bearded man said. "You can believe we'll massacre them Bambis in November."

"We'll shoot the bucks and fuck the does," the other man added.

"Don't get them mixed up," I said.

"Happy trails, chief."

After half an hour I cut away from the logging road and walked through a large field of marsh grass and cattails to the lakeshore. It was a circular lake of about fifty acres. Cattails and rice plants sprouted from the shallows. Early this morning the lake had smoked with the cold, and some Indians in a skiff had been gathering wild rice on the far shore. They bent the stalks over the skiff and beat the grains loose with sticks. At that distance, seen through the rising vapor, it had looked like murder. The Indians were gone now. It was silent except for some crows.

Harkey's cabin was primitive, a roughly hewn log hut that was hardly bigger than a garage, with an iron pipe chimney sticking out of the shake roof, tin and asphalt patches here and there, and nearby a NO TRESPASSING sign that had been riddled by bullets. In front of the cabin a crude wooden dock extended thirty feet into the lake.

I opened the padlock and entered the dim, musty cabin. Its windows were small and placed high on the east and west walls. There was a blackened Franklin stove in the center of the room, bunk beds stacked against a wall, a table and four chairs, bookshelves, a tall cabinet, a firewood box, and dirty throw rugs that looked like coiled ropes. The splintery floorboards and the logs had been crudely planed and the cracks caulked with a claylike substance. Overhead, a dozen peeled eight-inch logs served as rafters.

I lit both burners of the Coleman stove and put a pan of water on one of them. My hands were trembling. My legs were weak, and several times my left knee buckled. It was not just fatigue. I felt—not sick exactly, but soon to become sick, the way you feel a few hours before flu symptoms appear.

I made a cup of instant coffee with cream and sugar and sat down at the table with its knife scars and cigarette burns. Frozen drops of water in the room's cobwebs glowed like insects' eyes. The place was a pigsty. Harkey's "summer cottage." His old "hunting-fishing" camp.

I made another cup of coffee, put some bacon in a frying pan, and when it was sizzling added three eggs. It was ten minutes after noon. My jacket and trousers were stiff with blood. There were streaks of blood on my right hand and caked blood beneath the fingernails. In the mirror above the sink I saw that my face was freckled with blood. I pumped water into the sink and thoroughly scrubbed my hands and face. I was glad that I couldn't remember killing the man. That short blackout was like a kind of innocence.

I scooped the bacon and eggs out onto a tin plate, sliced and buttered two pieces of bread, spread them with orange marmalade, and sat down and ate. I was ravenous. That shamed me. I could imagine a prosecutor saying, "And so two hours after savagely murdering a man you sat down to a hearty meal of bacon and eggs and coffee." Yes.

A decision must be made soon, and it had to be the right one; that decision would eliminate every other possibility. That choice would lead to an ever more restrictive series of choices. At the end of the series I would be dead, imprisoned, or free.

I had to get out of the claustral cabin. Breathing here required conscious effort. I took my coffee outside and walked to the end of the dock. The water was clear. Silky green weeds, as fine and long as a woman's hair, moved gently with the current. I saw weeds, rocks, a beer can, snails and freshwater clams, a dead crayfish lying belly-up on the silty bottom. The lake smelled faintly of iron and fish. The surface dimpled with each snowflake.

Silence, falling snow, a delicate suspension. I was no one. My act of murder had divested both my victim and myself of identity. I had a name, a past, but no true self; that had evaporated like the mist, like the man's life. It was very strange. Nothing really existed for me except this acutely sensed present. A weathered, bleached pierpost seemed more real than I. Its whorled grain was a map that I could not quite read. Superreal, too, were the trees, the wrinkled texture of the lake's surface, the dead crab in the silt, the mothlike snowflakes, the dim luminosity of the clouds overhead. Each object was sharply separated from the other; there was no cohesiveness, no unity in the natural world. Each object, even light, was sinister in its isolation. Maybe this was how a child saw the world and then forget his seeing. Maybe this was how a psychotic saw the world.

A pair of mallard ducks emerged from a clump of reeds thirty yards away and paddled out into the lake. The drake's iridescent neck feathers seemed to burn in the dull, milky light. I watched the drake seize the hen's bill in his own and force her beneath the surface. He held her under for perhaps twenty seconds. I thought she might drown, but then he released her, she bobbed to the surface, and they paddled off together.

It was twelve-thirty. I felt very tired, incapable of action. Perhaps, if I could nap for half an hour . . .

I walked behind the cabin and brushed snow off my car. Five or six inches had fallen, and it was still coming down. The car had front wheel drive; I should have no trouble getting it up the twisty ruts to the paved highway. I switched on the radio and listened to a resonant voice talk about the war: logistics, tactics, casualties. There was always a war. After the news another voice reported on the weather: The surprise autumn storm had already left six inches of snow in northern Wisconsin, and another four to six inches was expected. The roads were snow-packed; driving was hazardous. The sheriff feared that some bow hunters might be lost in the woods. Hypothermia was a serious danger;

the temperature was expected to fall to ten degrees late tonight.

I trashed the cabin. Let them think vandals had broken in. I pried loose the padlock's hasp with the tire iron. I emptied the twelve cans of beer I'd brought down the sink and scattered them around the room. I urinated in a corner. What would they steal? The Coleman stove, the pressure lantern, fishing rods, a rusty old twelve-gauge shotgun, a down sleeping bag. I carried everything out, stuffed it into the trunk of the car, and returned to the cabin.

Snow was drifting in through the open door. I removed all of my clothes except my underwear, washed my hands, arms, and face again, then dressed in clean slacks, dress shirt, sweater, street shoes, and a sports coat. I had shaved this morning.

What else? I wiped every surface that I might have touched inside the cabin: pots and pans, utensils, the pump handle, the Franklin stove, the table, the beer cans, magazines, padlock and door handle, cups, glasses, everything.

I carried my bloody clothes, the knife with which I had killed Dempsey, and the supplies I'd brought from the city out to the car and packed them away in the truck.

What else? I was jittery, confused, fearful of forgetting something crucial. Could these hick cops be very efficient?

I returned to the cabin and stood in the center and looked carefully around. Had I wiped every surface that could preserve a print? Any personal objects remaining here? What else? It was ten minutes after one. What else? I did not want to leave the cabin. Finally I realized that I could remain here until night and still not eliminate my anxiety. My fear would not be left behind.

Leave the door open. Let the snow blow in. Snow was still thickly falling. Snow would cover my footprints and, with luck, the tire tracks. What else?

The town was crowded. Stocky Indian men lounged on street corners, indifferent to the falling snow. Indian children and crazy-eyed dogs rode in the beds of pickup trucks. Hunters walked in groups of three and four; most appeared as drunk as the street corner Indians. There was a festive mood in the town; the storm had liberated people—they were all truants this afternoon.

I stopped at a gas station at the edge of town and filled the tank from a self-service pump. It was warm and smoky inside. Wet woolen mittens were smoking on a heating vent. The cashier was an Indian youth with his long hair fastened in a ponytail. Stupidly I almost paid with a credit card. I asked him to return the card and paid in cash.

"How is the highway going south?" I asked.

"Not too good. But the snowplows and sanders are out now. You shouldn't have too much trouble if you drive carefully."

"That's what I'll do," I said.

It took me four hours to drive the first hundred miles, three hours for the second hundred, and ninety minutes for the third. I drove through the near-blizzard, through a freezing rain and sleet, then through a gentle rain, and finally, in the southern part of the state, I could see stars. I was not involved in an accident. The police did not stop me. An attendant at a gas station in Chicago told me that it had not snowed or rained there; it had, in fact, been a pleasant autumn day.

I parked my car on the street and in two trips carried everything up to my apartment on the sixth floor. The air was stale and smelled faintly of the damp ashes in the fireplace. It was a one-bedroom condo unit containing a Pullman kitchen, a dining alcove that I used as a study, and a living room with a slanted cedar beam ceiling. Beyond the sliding doors was a balcony big enough for two chairs, a circular table, and a couple of potted plants. The mortgage payments were more than I could afford. I was paying for the neighborhood and a view of the river.

The kitchen sink was filled with dirty dishes. There was nothing in the refrigerator that I cared to eat. I filled a glass with ice cubes, poured in some scotch, and carried it into the living room.

The digital clock on the mantel read 9:54, and turned to 9:55, 9:56, 9:57, 9:58, 9:59, 10:00. It seemed much later: three in the morning, four.

I was relieved to be home. I felt safe now, although my situation hardly justified the feeling. The future lacked definition. My freedom was provisional. I sensed within myself a vacancy. Perhaps it had always been there; maybe I had created it in those few savage minutes that I could not even remember. I had, in a way, ceased to be. But at the same time I felt the first faint stirrings of a radical new kind of freedom—a release from all my vows.

THREE

John Dempsey
TV Writer, Producer

John Dempsey, 44, creator of the popular television series *Hell's Precinct* and the author of more than fifty TV scripts, has died, his family said Thursday. The cause of death was not disclosed, and the family's statement did not reveal the date of death.

Mr. Dempsey, born in Chicago and a resident of the city for many years, was an original member of the experimental theater group Harlequinade before moving to California to continue his acting career there.

He appeared in dozens of television shows, including *Baker's Dozen; Adamoski and Evie; My Town, Your Town;* and the popular miniseries *The Sante Fe Trail,* before concentrating his efforts on writing and producing. Speaking of his acting career in a 1988 *People* magazine interview, he said, "I played good bad guys. Vulnerable psychopaths."

In 1984 the one-hour series he created and produced, *Hell's Precinct,* appeared on CBS television and was an immediate success with critics and viewers. The show collected nineteen Emmy nominations and eleven awards during its four years of network presentation.

Mr. Dempsey also wrote five original screenplays that were produced by major motion picture companies, and in 1989 he wrote and coproduced the controversial satirical comedy *Irish Babies,* which was picketed by fundamentalist religious groups in many U.S. cities before being withdrawn by its distributors. However, the movie was popular in Europe, where it received several prizes, including the Grand Prix at the Paris Film Festival.

Mr. Dempsey is survived by his wife, Claudia; his son, Dante; and his parents, Michael and Mavis Dempsey.

Visitation will be from 9 a.m. to noon Friday in the Sorrel Brothers Funeral Home at Clear Springs, Wisconsin. Internment at Foxhill Cemetery at 2 p.m. Friday.

FOUR

Clark Wheeler Crabbe's secretary regularly put food out on the window ledge for the pigeons. They danced in little circles, bobbing their heads, when she lifted the sash window and spread the bread crumbs and seed. She burbled and cooed like the birds. "There you are, my angels," she said. She closed the window and returned to her desk, saying, "It's a very nasty day, Mr. Neville. The air smells like rusty iron. It smells like a hard winter coming on, sir."

"Yes," I said.

"And what did you say you wished to see Mr. Crabbe about?"

"It's a confidential matter, Mrs. O'Malley."

"Very well," she said. "Indeed."

I could hear traffic noises rising from the street nine floors below. It was still raining. The pigeons were blurry behind the rain-smeared window. They were old flawed panes that distorted light even when clean and dry. The bare radiators clanked. This was an old suite of offices in a very old building. The furniture was heavy and old. The hardwood floors had been restored and were highly polished. There were Daumier prints on the walls: pompous judges and venal lawyers in their pleated gowns, greedy swine-faced men cutting deals.

Mrs. O'Malley sniffed and dabbed a wad of tissue paper to her nostrils. The radiators clanked. I looked at the cartoons in a copy of *The New Yorker.* Now and then I glanced through the window at the blurry pigeons and the broken spectrum beyond. Someone was shouting unintelligibly down on the street, a taxi driver or cop or madman.

Then the big oak door opened and Clark came out. I rose and we shook hands. He took my arm and guided me into his office. It was a big space: there was a wall of leather-bound law books, a row of old sash windows overlooking the street, a desk that looked like it had been whittled out of a solid block of mahogany, and stained and cracked leather chairs and sofa. The carpet was faded and the intricate pattern worn away in places.

"Andrew," he said. "Damned good to see you. You look more like your father every day. But I see your mother, too—in your eyes, son, and a little around your mouth."

I waited until he was seated behind his desk, and then I lowered myself into a leather chair. There were other Daumier prints in this room. I saw a small oxygen tank and mask in the corner.

Clark had gained weight since I'd last seen him. He was a big overweight man with a red face and silky white hair. There were webs of broken blood vessels on his nose and cheeks. His eyes were murky.

"I'm sorry I didn't visit you in the hospital, Clark," I said.

"Ah, well, shit, buddy—who likes hospitals? Flowers, graveyard faces, 'how're ya doing,' 'get well soon,' all that horseshit. Hospitals, mortuary chapels, cemeteries, all of the mandated hypocrisy. They cut some veins out of my legs and sutured them to my heart. The heart's not pleased with the new arrangement, I can tell. How is your sister?"

"Fran is fine."

"She has two kids now? Three?"

"Three."

"Her husband still a jerk?"

"Still a jerk."

"All right, Andrew. You're in trouble. Tell me about it."

"I killed a man," I said.

His expression did not change. "How?"

"With a knife. I stabbed him. Many times."

"When did this occur?"

"Six days ago."

"Where?"

"In northern Wisconsin, near Eagle's Nest."

"Who was this man?"

"He was a stranger at the time. But I knew him years ago and had forgotten him. His name was John Dempsey. I have some news clippings from the *Milwaukee Journal* and an obituary from the *Tribune.*" I removed the clippings from my breast pocket, unfolded them, and passed them to Crabbe.

"And you've come to me because the police suspect you?"

"No. I've heard nothing from the police."

"Why did you kill the man, Andrew?"

"It was about a deer. I believed that he was stealing the deer I killed. And he had a knife."

"Did he threaten you with his knife?"

"No. Maybe; I'm not certain. But I don't think so."

Crabbe spread the newspaper clippings out on his desk and quickly read them. He looked up.

"A prominent man," he said.

"Yes."

"Where and when did you know him?"

"Here, in Chicago. We were members of the same theater group. We were friendly but not friends. I knew him for a year, and then he left for California. I never saw him after that."

"Until a week ago in Wisconsin. You say you didn't recognize him?"

"No. It was a long time ago. Twenty years ago, twenty-one."

"Did you like Dempsey?"

"Yes. He was energetic, cheerful, funny."

"Did you envy him, Andrew?"

"No."

"Had he changed a great deal in the twenty years?"

"No, not really. No more than I. He didn't recognize me, either."

"How do you know?"

"He would have said something, wouldn't he?"

"Andrew. Shit. Would you like a drink?"

"Yes, please."

Crabbe got up and walked over to a cabinet.

"Scotch," I said. "No ice, no water."

He returned and placed the glass on the edge of his desk. "I can't drink with you. The doctors."

"Then I shouldn't smoke."

"No, go ahead; light up. I can't smoke anymore, but I like the smell."

He waited until I'd lit the cigarette, and then he said, "Now you're going to tell me all about it. Give me a strictly factual account of the incident. I don't want to hear about how you felt, what you thought, what might have occurred—tell me only what happened."

"All right."

"Tell me about it as if you were not a participant, just an invisible bystander."

I nodded.

"And after the objective version I want you to tell me your subjective view. What you thought, felt, suspected, dreamed. And after that you will tell me once more, blending the factual and the subjective versions. All right? Go ahead, Andrew."

I told my story three times, as Crabbe had instructed, and was surprised by how different each version sounded. It was the same event all three times, but the implications were contradictory, the essence concealed. I had not lied. The truth was more elusive than I had supposed.

"Now tell me the story from the viewpoint of the victim—John Dempsey."

I sat quietly for a long time, looking through the rain-smeared window. The film of water broke the outdoors into incoherent blobs of color, as a drastically out-of-focus camera might.

"I can't," I said.

"You can't tell me the story from Dempsey's point of view?"

"No."

"Later then, perhaps. Think about it and when you are ready tell me—or tell yourself—the victim's story."

"All right."

"Where did you buy the hunting license?"

"I didn't have one. I really didn't intend to go hunting. My thought was just to get out of the city for a long weekend. Walk in the woods, reflect, rest. I've been very tired lately, exhausted. I needed the time off, the isolation. But when I got up early Saturday morning I saw the bow and the quiver of arrows hanging on the wall of the cabin, and I thought, Well, I'll take them along. Maybe I'll see a deer. It was an impulse. A whim. Really, I just went for an early-morning walk in the fog."

"But you had a knife."

"Yes, a sheath knife I found in the cabin. It had a bone handle and a blade about seven inches long."

"You wanted the knife in the event you killed a deer?"

"Well, no. I didn't think about it clearly. I was sleepy and had no definite purpose in mind. I just put the sheath on my belt and carried along the bow and quiver of arrows."

"Okay," he said.

"Don't you believe it?"

"I do believe it. It's perfectly ordinary. All of us are only half-conscious most of the time. We're vague. We act without clear purpose. I believe you, Andrew, but no jury would."

"I understand."

"You said there was a lake. Did you buy a fishing license?"

"No."

"And so you drove straight from Chicago to Eagle's Nest on

Friday night, and after the incident on Saturday you drove straight back to the city. You didn't stay at a motel or use a credit card or buy a sporting license or get stopped by police for a traffic violation."

"No, none of those things."

"There are no documents floating around Wisconsin, then. How long were you out of the city?"

"I left work early on Friday. Say four o'clock. I left the city at four, arrived at the cabin a little after midnight, I think, and returned Saturday. I was back in my place at about ten Saturday night. So, say thirty hours."

"And you told no one of your plans for the weekend. Not even this Mr. Harkey, the owner of the cabin."

"No."

"No one."

"No one."

"Do you have a telephone answering machine, Andrew?"

"Yes."

"Did you leave a recorded message saying that you would be out of town for the weekend?"

"I did, yes, but when I checked the machine Saturday night there were no messages, not even a hang-up."

"The Indians whom you saw gathering wild rice on the lake—do you think they could identify you?"

"It was very foggy, and they were some distance away. I wouldn't be able to identify them."

"And the two hunters you met? They could identify you?"

"Yes."

"Andrew, did you think about going to the police?"

"Yes. I decided against it because of the . . . brutality of the killing. The violence and senselessness of it. It was murder."

"They don't have the death penalty in Wisconsin."

"I know."

"If you'd gone to the police . . ."

"I couldn't."

"Dempsey attacked you; you fought back. Cop a plea for involuntary manslaughter. Three years, Andrew, five, six . . ."

"No. I could not survive in prison."

"So you decided against surrendering to the police. You decided to immediately return to Chicago. Did you consider remaining there for the entire weekend as you'd planned? To go on as if you hadn't killed a man?"

"No. I couldn't. I knew . . . if the body were found that weekend—I knew that if the police questioned me I would collapse. I'd crack. I couldn't have dealt with the pressure then. I had to run."

"And now, Andrew? If the police questioned you now?"

"I'm stronger now."

"Have you ever been fingerprinted?"

"No."

"No military service, no job that required fingerprinting, no arrests when the police took your prints?"

"No."

"What did you do with the objects you removed from the cabin? Your bloody clothing, the knife, the other things?"

"I burned everything that would burn and threw everything else into various sections of the river."

"Are you sure that you didn't tell this Mr. Harkey that you intended to use his cabin that weekend?"

"I didn't mention it to anyone. It was an open offer. Last summer, in July or August, he told me that he owned a primitive cabin in Wisconsin and I was welcome to use it anytime. He told me where the key was hidden. I said, 'Well, maybe I'll drive up there sometime.' It was vague. We haven't discussed the cabin since."

"You impulsively decided to drive up there for the weekend. You were exhausted. You needed rest, isolation. Has Mr. Harkey mentioned the murder? It received attention in the newspapers, and it happened in the vicinity of his cabin."

"No, he hasn't said anything."

"The vandalism of his cabin?"

"No, no mention."

"You arrived back in the city at around ten o'clock Saturday night. What did you do then?"

"I cleaned up and telephoned a woman I know—Jenny Welles—and asked her if she wanted to go out for a drink. She said yes. We went to a couple of bars and then had a late dinner."

"So Jenny Welles and others—acquaintances, bartenders, waiters—can establish that you were in the city Saturday night. Was that your intention in asking her out?"

"Yes."

"Would you like another drink, Andrew?"

"No, thank you."

"I'm going to have one. I wish you hadn't brought this to me. I wish you had gone to a priest or psychiatrist. Their kind of confidentiality covers situations like this. The attorney-client privilege does not. Not in a case like this. Are you sure you won't have another scotch?"

"I will, yes."

He returned with the drinks and said, "And I'll have one of your cigarettes, too."

He did not talk to me, he did not look at me, until he had finished his drink and the cigarette.

"All right. You say you do not recall the actual killing."

"I remember the deer and all the blood on the snow, and I remember Dempsey reaching for his knife."

"Presumably to finish cleaning the deer?"

"I suppose. And then there is an absolute blank until I awakened some time later. That's what it was like—waking up after a refreshing nap."

"Andrew, ninety-nine percent of the stories of blackouts, episodes of amnesia during the commission of a felony, are pure and simple horseshit. Juries smile when they hear that crap."

"I don't care. It happened to me. I am not lying."

"Andrew, you aren't epileptic, are you?"

"No."

"You've never been diagnosed as suffering from psychomotor epilepsy?"

"No. Of course not. There's nothing wrong with my brain."

"Well, have you ever experienced anything that could be described as a seizure? I don't mean a fall-down convulsion. I mean something like lapses in cognition, temporary dreamlike states that might last only a few minutes, seconds even. Do you ever have difficulty recalling a recent event?"

"No, nothing like that. I'm not *sick,* Clark."

"No occasional sense of strangeness, a disassociation from people and events, a sense of absurdity as you observe yourself performing some ordinary task? I mean a sense of wrongness, of things being remote, not right, strange?"

"No."

"No amnesia ever?"

"No."

"Did you ever suffer a serious head injury? A concussion?"

"No, for Christ's sake, no."

"Andrew, I'm your godfather. I've known you since we met at the baptismal font." His quick smile was like a flinch of pain. "Your father was my best friend. I've known you all your life. Your life until now—until a week ago—has been quiet, honest, decent."

"Mediocre."

"And then, then—my God—and then you suddenly contradict, you repudiate, the values of a lifetime, the life itself, the life you've lived, yourself."

"Quiet, honest, decent."

"Don't mock me. I want to know how you feel about savagely killing this poor man. A good-enough man, apparently. What do you feel?"

"I don't remember killing him."

"You've been candid so far. Do you now deny killing him?"

"No. I killed him. But I don't feel anything yet. I know what I should say. I know the words. Guilt, remorse, pity. Pity for the man and his devastated family. 'I am so sorry.' 'I will never do it again.' 'I will somehow make up for my brutal crime.' 'I can't sleep.' Terrible anguish. 'I've found God.' 'I intend to devote the rest of my life to good works.' But the truth is, Clark, the truth is, so far I've felt absolutely nothing. Zero. I feel no more for Dempsey than I do for the deer I killed."

"You feel fear," Crabbe said. "That's why you've come to see me today. You do, at least, feel fear."

"Yes."

"Andrew . . ."

"It will be all right. I need time. I'm still in shock, I think. I'm sure that in time I'll feel the appropriate emotions, and the appropriate emotions will lead to the appropriate deed."

"You've put me in a terrible position, Andrew."

"I see that now."

"For the record, I must advise you to go to the police. I'll accompany you."

I shook my head.

"All right."

"I need time."

"Write me a check for five dollars," he said.

I filled out the check and gave it to him.

"I can't charge my usual fee, Andrew. First, because you are my godson. That seems to mean nothing nowadays, but it was a responsibility I seriously accepted. It was a vow. But also, this is not a case I would accept for any amount of money. You have involved me."

"That wasn't my intention."

"If you are contacted by the police say nothing. Nothing. Phone me here or at my home. Don't try to fool the police. Don't believe that you can placate them by cooperating. Don't affect innocence or attempt to persuade. Shut up. Call me."

"I will."

"Don't act like an innocent man, Andrew. Behave like a guilty man. Say nothing. Don't accept a cigarette or a cup of coffee from the cops. Don't tell them the color of your eyes. Call me."

"I understand," I said.

FIVE

Foxhill was an old cemetery on a remote country road. Some of the monuments dated from the 1840s. Oaks and maples were scattered around the cemetery, and their roots had tilted and overturned many of the granite stones. The uncut grass was thick with leaves and burr thistles. Four acres were enclosed by a rusty iron spear fence; the main gate was askew on its hinges. Dead leaves had thickly drifted into the eastern fence line and now crackled dryly in the wind. The land beyond the fence was cut into a patchwork of corn- and wheat fields and pasture and dark clusters of trees. Far to the west I could see a farmhouse and barn with its twin concrete silos.

I walked a narrow dirt path that tacked here and there among the monuments. Nearly all of the graves were level with the earth or slightly depressed. Few had been tended. I saw only one bouquet of withered flowers. There were some empty beer cans on the dew-wet grass, a crumpled cigarette package, and a condom that looked like some translucent undersea thing—a jellyfish, a tubeworm.

Half a dozen yards away was an excavated pit, a steep-sided rectangle about seven feet long and deep and perhaps four feet wide. Dempsey's grave. It was filled to the brim with shadow at this early hour. The first eighteen inches were black topsoil, then a layer of gravelly earth, several feet of moist gray clay, and then crumbly reddish dirt filled with chalky stones. You could see sheared-off roots in the dirt walls, some as fine as silk thread, others thicker than my arm. It would not take long for the roots to penetrate and crack open Dempsey's coffin.

I picked the thistles off my socks and trouser legs, returned to the car, and drove down cambered country roads through villages blue with smoke. Children were walking and bicycling to school. Leaves burned in the gutters. The air smelled of leaf smoke and apples.

The body was available for viewing from nine in the morning until noon. I arrived thirty minutes early and had to be admitted by an employee. I watched as he lit all of the candles and opened the coffin lid. He removed a small tube from his pocket and sprayed the air. Then he stood on a chair and removed a crucifix from the back wall.

"It will be a secular service," he said.

It was a narrow, high room with a vaulted ceiling and a Gothic stained-glass window on the east wall. There was wine-red carpeting, velvet drapes, fancy gilt filigree on the cornices, and candelabra that burned in wall niches and in tiers behind the catafalque.

"Are you a member of the family"

"A friend."

"It's a very sad thing."

"I'm surprised the coffin will be open."

"You mean. Yes. But there was very little decay because of the cold weather. Hunters found the remains, you know."

"Yes."

"And the remains were not mutilated by rodents or birds. So, you see, there really was no difficulty in restoring the remains."

"I understand."

"It's a very sad thing," he said again as he left the room.

The casket rested on a platform at the rear of the chapel; you mounted three carpeted steps at the right, passed the length of the casket, and then descended three more steps to room level.

I could smell candlewax and brass polish and deodorant spray and, very faintly, the odor of corruption.

The box was ebony with brass carrying rods and hinges and a padded silk lining. Even the underside of the lid was lined. Dempsey's head rested on a little silk pillow.

His hair and mustache had been trimmed and combed. Color had been applied to his lips and cheeks. His skin had a glossy sheen, like new scar tissue. He was not smiling, but his mouth had been arranged in a way that suggested a smile was imminent. He was not wearing his glasses.

There was a cream-white display handkerchief in the breast pocket of his suit. I removed it. It was a very fine silk. No monogram. I refolded the handkerchief along its original creases and placed it in my own breast pocket. I regarded this act as like seizing the flag of a vanquished enemy.

There were a dozen cars parked alongside the road when I returned to the cemetery at two o'clock. Clusters of people strolled along the path. I left my car and passed through the unhinged gate and onto the grounds. Steep sunlight incandesced the autumn leaves and cast dark broken shadows. The wind tumbled dead leaves over the ground. Crackling, they drifted against the monuments and tree trunks and iron spear fence.

A man, dressed in a black suit and white shirt with a black tie but wearing jogging shoes, walked among the tombstones while listening to a cassette recorder through earphones. His hair was tied in a ponytail. He was darkly tanned. A blond woman nearby said, "Josh? I think it's starting now, Josh." The wind ballooned her skirt. "Josh?"

People in groups of two and three were drifting toward the grave. The massive ebony coffin was poised on the rim of the pit. Its brass burned white-gold in the sunlight. I walked that way. Ahead, I saw the widow. She was at the center of the *tableau vivant* that was now forming around her. A small boy held her hand. Dante. He looked very much like his father; he had the same eyes and mouth and a similar look of mischief.

On their left stood an old couple: she was stout; he was thin and stooped; both of their faces were sour with age and resentment and sorrow. I could sense their disapproval at thirty yards.

The widow was a proud woman. She'd remained aware. She had not sought a blind inner refuge from the confusion and pain. She refused to be victimized by her suffering (or the old couple on her left). Her gaze was clear and direct, and it parried my own rude stare.

On her right was a tall man with white hands and brown hair cut in a sort of street urchin style. The haircut made him appear young from a distance, but as I approached I saw that he was in his middle forties. His face, like his long-fingered hands, was very white, nearly albino white. His lips were moist and red, and so were the membranes around his eyes. He had a vague, whimsical air, as if he were in a theater or gallery and not at graveside. Now he hunched his narrow shoulders and murmured something to the widow.

She wore a black wool suit with a long skirt, black stockings, black gloves, black shoes. The wisps of hair that escaped her scarf were dark with silvery glints where touched by sunlight. Her eyes were a greenish-gray. I was not prepared for her beauty. It wounded.

The man called Josh and the woman who had spoken to him and a few others—friends of Dempsey's from Los Angeles—gathered around the grave. Josh glanced at his watch; a man with a pageboy haircut closed his eyes and deeply inhaled the air's fragrance; a woman stared sulkily down into the pit.

I saw an odd thuggish character who wore a nubby oat-colored sport coat and baggy gray slacks. He wore black brogues without socks. He had short arms and legs. His torso was thick, round, and his head looked as round as a cannonball resting on a thick, wattled neck. He was bald except for patches of thistly hair. His small moist blue eyes flicked here and there, and when he saw me he grinned insolently.

I saw the man who had admitted me to the mortuary chapel this morning; he was dressed in a shiny black suit, and his black hair had been greased back in a pompadour. He looked like a crow. There were crows and owls and jays and dusty sparrows gathered here today.

A few stragglers arrived and all—thirty-five or forty of us—were gathered around the grave. The boy peered quizzically down into the pit. His mother squeezed his hand

The tall, pale man removed half-lense reading glasses from his breast pocket and fussily adjusted them low on his nose. His skin was rough, like curdled milk, and his lips looked bloody against the whiteness.

The boy glanced at the box that contained his father's corpse, down into the pit, up at his mother, and then again at the coffin. His expression changed from curiosity to outrage.

The eulogist began: "I feel greatly honored to have been called 'friend' by John Dempsey, for 'friend' was not a word he used carelessly; it implicitly and generously assumed that you shared his ideals of friendship, his magnanimous nature, his extraordinary sense of responsibility toward his friends; that, in fact, you were capable of reciprocating his love in equal measure.

"I am honored, too, more than I can—"

Earlier I had noticed hundreds of blackbirds gathering in a nearby cornfield, flocking for their migration south. They were madly excited. They rose in spinning clouds like dust devils and then settled back again. Then all at once, while the eulogist spoke, they rose, swarming and chittering, in a black swirl and flew into the cemetery, where they perched in the oaks and maples. There was great noise and confusion. White bird mute rained down from the trees. The clothes of some of the mourners were spattered. Josh had white bird shit in his hair. The widow was trying not to smile. And then, just as abruptly, the birds swirled away to the west.

"I am honored, too, more than I can say, by John's lovely wife, who asked me to speak on behalf of all of us today, to help bid farewell to the lover, the husband, the father, the good and kind and honest man—our friend."

The old couple—Dempsey's mother and father—stared contemptuously at the eulogist. The lines on their faces were like the lines a caricaturist might use to express bitterness and scorn.

"In Plato's *Symposium* we are privileged to listen while Socrates and others speak about love. Socrates, Aristophanes, Alcibiades, the playwright Agathon, and others, they discuss the many kinds of love, the lower and the higher, and we hear—"

A gust of wind ripped through the trees and snatched a page from the man's hand. It sailed half the length of the cemetery, landed, flew again, and then tumbled to the iron fence, where it halted in a drift of leaves.

After a moment of hesitation the eulogist said, "Oh, we know; John did that! He is laughing at my pomposity." And then, his voice lower and more resonant, he said, "All right, John, you win again. I'll speak extempore and less grandly." He lifted his white hand, spread his fingers, and let the wind carry away the remaining two pages.

The stocky, thuggish man gradually drifted away from the gathering, and then, believing himself unobserved, he turned abruptly and began walking toward the gate. He was mostly torso and head, like an ape. Short arms, short bowed legs, and a clumsy rolling gait. Even so, there was something jaunty in his stride. Just beyond the fence he paused to drink deeply from a pint bottle. He slapped his chest.

The eulogist was talking as grandly as before about his "protégé" John Dempsey: he had early on spotted John's talent . . . his—"I dare say it, his genius. A genius, alas, that now can never be fully realized." He had an actor's trained voice, and he used it cynically.

The thug was walking along the shoulder of the road. He passed several parked cars, stopped next to my own, peered in through the side window for a moment, then opened the door and slid inside.

I backed away from the grave. The widow looked at me. I could not read her expression. A few strands of hair were blown obliquely across her cheek. She gazed into my eyes for a time and then shifted her attention to the silk handkerchief in my pocket.

I walked through a drift of leaves and out the gate. A puff of smoke emerged from my car's window.

He was sitting in the driver's seat. The glove box was open, and he was looking through the mail and receipts he'd found there.

"Couldn't take any more of that old queen's oratory either, huh, pal?"

"What are you doing?"

"Andrew C. Neville. What kind of name is Neville—that French? Look here. This envelope. You didn't even open it. It's from a collection agency. The miserable scuts. You owe $647.49. They're talking litigation. Pay your fucking bills, Andrew. Stop being a deadbeat."

"There's a funeral in progress," I said. "That's why I haven't dragged you out of my car and punched your ugly face."

"Hey, hey, whoa, you make it sound easy. It ain't that easy."

His breath reeked of whiskey and tobacco. There was a rash like prickly heat on his scalp and neck.

"And look at this. Give me a fucking break, Andrew. Old parking tickets. That's how it starts. You don't pay your parking tickets. You don't pay legitimate debts. Then you steal a newspaper from the blind man at the post office. Then you cop a feel in the elevator. Next you rob, you rape, you kill, you mutilate."

"Who are you?"

"Roland Scheiss is the name."

"Scheiss means 'shit' in German, doesn't it?"

He plucked the cigar from between his teeth and laughed. His teeth were small and spaced like baby teeth. "Close, but not quite, Andrew. Now, my friend, if you'll step back, I'll exit your vehicle. Be fair—don't sucker punch me when I'm half-in, half-out. Don't kick me in the balls. Be nice."

He got out of the car and walked past me to the rear. He had taken the keys from the ignition. "I'm always ascared to open a trunk," he said. "Englishers call it the boot. I opened a boot once and found intimate body parts. Not nice."

The funeral was breaking up now. People were drifting away from the grave.

Scheiss lifted the trunk lid. "Nope." He crossed himself. "Thank the triune God. My heart is wildly pounding, Andrew. But no body parts, no curious stains or implements. The tire's a little soft. Bring it up to about thirty-two psi next time you happen by a service station."

He slammed the trunk lid shut and tossed the keys in the air.

I caught them.

"I like to see who comes to a murdered man's funeral."

He was six or seven inches shorter than me, but I guessed that our weights were about equal.

He smiled, stuck the cigar between his teeth, turned, and sauntered away.

I returned to the cemetery. The wind was blowing very hard now. Tree limbs clattered and leaves swarmed over the ground. There were no clouds: the sky was a bright, clean wind-washed blue. The crowd had broken into small groups. The widow and her son, the eulogist, and the funeral director were standing near the grave. She saw me looking at her, saw me approaching, and separated from her group. We met near a granite obelisk.

"I'm sorry," I said. "I'm very sorry."

"Thank you."

"My name is Andrew Neville."

"You were a friend of John's?" She spoke with an Italian accent.

"Yes."

"I don't recall hearing your name."

"It was a long time ago."

She nodded.

"I wanted to be here. I apologize if I intruded."

"Is that John's handkerchief?"

"Yes."

"I thought so. I noticed this morning that it was gone."

"Yes, I took it."

"I bought six of them for John this spring. They're silk, from Italy."

"It's . . . very nice."

"Why did you take the handkerchief from his pocket?"

"I don't know."

"You don't know?"

"I really don't. It was an impulse."

"Did you want it as a memento of John?"

"I don't know."

"Some of us will be going to my house now. There will be food and drink. Would you like to come?"

"Yes. Thank you."

"Do you know the way?"

"No."

"Follow that car, the Mercedes."

"All right."

"Very well, then."

SIX

I joined a convoy led by the black Mercedes-Benz. My car was last in line. Roland Scheiss drove the car directly ahead. Dempsey's parents sat in the rear, and every now and then the old man twisted around to stare back at me.

We drove several miles through a grid of cornfields to a narrow county road, south for five minutes, and then down a long, curving hill into a smoky village of frame houses and ancient trees. The procession turned left and down a village road littered with leaves and twigs and fallen walnuts. After five blocks the road hooked south and on my left was the lake, slate-green and choppy in the wind. Spray misted on the windshield. There were several piers with boats slotted alongside, and offshore more boats twisted and plunged against their moorings.

Mr. Dempsey looked back at me. His profile was vulturine. His wife looked rather like a bulldog. Roland Scheiss's eyes were reflected in his rearview mirror.

We passed restaurants and bars and shops, a park, a boat warehouse, a beach, crossed a bridge to the right of which were a protected harbor and a sprawling resort hotel, and then the road curved left as it rose into the low hills. The road continued east, climbing and descending a series of wooded hills, then leveled for a stretch. I saw big houses back in the trees and glimpses of the spume-flecked lake.

The widow lived about halfway down the south shore of the

twelve-mile-long lake, at the loop end of a driveway that snaked down through a ferny woods. A creek spanned at intervals by arched stone footbridges ran parallel to the driveway. I saw a small frame house off to my left, probably the caretaker's place, and scattered farther down a small greenhouse with fogged glass, a tennis court, and a gazebo circled by flower gardens.

Ahead and below was the house. It did not look special at this distance, this perspective: a blocky white stucco building with green shutters and trim, three red brick chimneys spaced along the roof peak, and a porte cochere supported by fluted white columns. Virginia creeper climbed the latticed walls. The house was not special except for its size: you could fit three or four ordinary houses beneath that roof.

We passed a man who was burning a tree stump. The fire had escaped into the grass, and a ring of transparent orange flame glowed through the smoke. He wore a dirty gray jumpsuit and rubber boots. He leaned on a rake and stared aggressively at each passing car.

The Mercedes stopped beneath the porte cochere, and Mrs. Dempsey and Dante got out. The other cars pulled off onto a paved area in front of the garages. They were garages now, but I thought that they might have been stables and a coach house a long time ago.

I parked between Scheiss's Buick and a BMW driven by the eulogist. Both had Illinois license plates.

The wind was moistened and cooled as it swept across the lake. I could hear the percussion of waves striking the shore. Big tree limbs swayed and clattered. It was blowing even harder now, gale force, though the sky remained clear.

Scheiss, standing with Dempsey's parents, repeatedly rubbed his scalp with both palms, as if smoothing his thistly hair. He saw me watching him and grinned swiftly, then thrust out both fists, one with the thumb up and the other with the thumb pointing down.

Everyone stood around awkwardly for a time and then began drifting toward the back door.

I remained behind. It was a rare sky, turquoise-green around the horizon deepening to turquoise-blue overhead. I inhaled the fresh wind. This was the first moment since early morning that the insidious stink of decay had left my nostrils. I no longer smelled Dempsey.

"You don't remember me, do you, Neville?"

I turned. It was the eulogist. I thought he had left with the others. He advanced. The wind had not seemed to muss his shaggy street urchin haircut. His face was long and bony and pale. Only his ears, the membranes around his eyes, and his moist lips were pink. His eyes were a rare luminous lavender color—contact lenses.

"It was a nice eulogy," I said.

He laughed. "You lie! I thought it was a beautiful eulogy, even better than Pericles' funeral oration—but I know that *you* would never think so."

"I'm sorry, but I don't recall . . ."

"Laddy Rawling." He stooped and stared into my eyes, then straightened. "Good Lord, you *don't* remember. I thought you were snubbing me. Laddy Rawling, Andrew. The Harlequinade theater group. Oh, really, you can't have forgotten. . . . This is cruel and absurd. Well then, imagine me at twenty-two, slender and freckled, lithe and seductive, impertinent. Puck. Don't you remember my Puck?"

"Ah," I said.

"Ah," he repeated, nodding and smiling.

I remembered him as a very bright and energetic young man who was continually fomenting little insurrections against the senior members of the company, abortive coups. He was then a gossip, a charming schemer, a backstage politician.

"So," I said. "How are you, Laddy?"

"Simply wretched, old boy. I grow old; I grow old; I shall wear my condoms rolled."

"Are you still involved in the theater?"

"Indirectly, almost clandestinely. I have become an éminence grise, Andrew. A power behind the scenes. It suits me well. Actually, I should have been a spy, a double agent, but being an éminence grise suits me nearly as well."

"What does a gray eminence do these days?" I asked.

"We administer, invest, and disperse the funds of filthy rich foundations, of course. I myself am the chairman of the Braddock Foundation. We patronize the performing arts. The legitimate theater mostly, but also needy opera and ballet companies. I have leverage, Andrew, power. I get my way. I whisper in the warty ear of my mistress, Helen O. Braddock, the only surviving child of the sausage king, and she says, 'As you wish, Laddy.' "

"Well, you look prosperous."

"As I should. Must."

We strolled toward the house.

"Now you," he said.

"Nothing to tell."

"Why did you stop writing?"

"Why do you assume that I've stopped?"

"Andrew, I know *everything* that goes on in the theater. What in the world have you been doing all these years?"

We reached the porte cochere and paused.

"Waiting," I said. I pressed the bell button. Chimes faintly echoed.

"Waiting for what?"

"I don't know," I said. "For today, maybe."

A woman who wore a frilly apron over a gray dress opened the door and beckoned. We followed her through a utility room and down a wide hallway and then through a carved oak door into a formal dining room. The carpet was old but still bright; its dominant color was indigo, with intricate designs in vermilion and saffron and cerulean. There was a mahogony refectory table with its sixteen high-backed chairs in place. It was a big room, and there was space enough for a china cabinet, a silver cabinet, a crystal cabinet, and, near a door that led into the kitchen, an elaborate serving station. Damask drapes hung the length of the wall on my left, and through a slit I could see leaded windows.

The woman led us through an arch and into a room so enormous that it was disorienting. The furnishings and people were dwarfed by space. It was mostly empty space from the hardwood floor—color-spotted here and there with Oriental rugs—to the blackened rafters three stories above. Smoke-fogged shafts of light, looking as solid as crystal, angled down from the high windows and shattered on the polished floor. I saw Scheiss and the old couple, the Californians, some others who had been at the cemetery, but I did not see the widow or her son.

"I'll get us a drink," Laddy said. "Scotch?"

"Fine."

There was a bar set up against the wall and next to it a buffet table.

Scheiss saw me and showed his knowing, sly grin. He held a fuming cigar in his left hand—I could smell it halfway across the room—and held a tumber of whiskey in his right. He said something to the old couple, and they turned and stared coldly at me.

Laddy arrived with my drink. "Excuse me, old boy," he said. "I'm going off to talk to some of these Hollywood zits."

The furniture was old and somewhat worn but of excellent quality. There were sofas and chairs—leather- and cloth-covered—coffee tables, the crescent-shaped bar with its brass rail and decorative spittoons, old, intricately carved chests and cabinets, the worn Oriental carpets scattered around. There was enough furniture to fill several ordinary rooms, but here it just seemed to exaggerate the space. No piece matched another piece, but they all seemed to belong, each in its present position, just so. Against the east wall, mounted on a three-step platform, there was an organ whose shiny brass pipes climbed the wall to varying heights.

Scheiss, a few yards away, said, "Some joint, hey, Andrew? There's the filthy rich and then there's us dirty poor."

I intended to pass by, but then he said, "You know John's ma and pa, don't you?"

"We haven't met."

"No? This here is Michael Dempsey, and the lady is John's ma, Mavis."

The old man pretended not to see my offered hand.

"I'm very sorry about your son," I said.

"When and where did you know John?" the woman asked.

"We met in the late seventies. We were both members of Harlequinade."

"I don't remember you."

"We never met, Mrs. Dempsey."

"That's exactly right," the old man said.

"We knew all of John's Chicago friends," she said. "All of his *good* friends. He used to bring them home to meet us. We always knew who his friends were."

"Maybe he didn't regard me as a friend," I said.

"Then why are you here?"

"The widow invited me. I believe this is her house." I nodded and left them.

"See you, Andrew," Scheiss said to my back.

There were big semioval bay windows on either side of the front door that extended eight or ten feet beyond the house's facade. I entered the bay on the right. Here the floor was parquet, with a throw rug, and there were matched chairs with a low table between them. On the table was an Indian pot containing a spray of fresh flowers, an ashtray, a lighter, and a box of cigarettes. I took one of the cigarettes and lit it.

The drapes were pulled and I could look down the undulating lawn to the wild green lakeshore. Foam lay in long parallel stripes over the waves. At the end of the flagstone walk was a terrace enclosed by iron railings, and steps leading down to the pier. The T-shaped pier extended well out into the lake. Two boats, one power- and one sail-, reared and plunged against their lines. Off to the right, half-concealed among some trees, was a small white building that I supposed was the boathouse.

"Beautiful, isn't it? In a miniature way?"

It was the Californian called Josh. He had released his blond hair from the ponytail, and now it flowed loosely to his shoulders. He was around forty, my height, and wore a tiny gold stud in his left ear.

"Miniature?" I said.

"When you live fifty yards from the Pacific Ocean, a lake this size looks like a facsimile of an ocean—special effects. When you're used to looking at redwoods, these oaks and maples look like shrubs. When you're used to mountains like the Sierras, these hills . . . I feel squeezed here. Everything looks squeezed beneath this sky. One of the villages we passed through—it was like the kind of thing you'd arrange at the base of your Christmas tree."

"You're saying this ain't California."

He nodded and smiled. "Yeah. Well, it ain't."

"Right. Small lakes, small trees, small hills, small towns, small people."

"That isn't what I meant."

"Sorry."

"Even so, I could never understand why John left the West Coast for a place like this. Still can't. Why would he leave the center of the business?"

"Maybe he figured that he had enough money."

"After a certain point the money isn't important except as an indicator of position and power. No, it's the game. It's like John left the game in the third quarter."

"Well," I said, "he's dead."

"Laddy Rawling pointed you out. I thought I'd say hello. Your *Let them Dance* was the first play I directed. I was a kid. This was at the La Jolla Playhouse. It's a good play. So are *Payback* and the three one-acters. I haven't read the others."

"There weren't any others."

"Laddy said you had stopped writing."

"You don't have to listen to Laddy."

"Then you're still writing? If you are, I'd very much like to see anything you have."

"For a film? Television?"

"No, the stage. I want to return to the theater for a year or two. It's the only way to be taken seriously."

"Why ask me for a play? There are thousands of manuscripts floating around."

"And they're all crap. Every one that I've had the misfortune to read. Pretentious, semiliterate. Pity and suffering. Oh, Jesus, the anguish—the anguish of AIDS, the anguish of racism, the anguish of failure, the anguish of marriage, the anguish of three generations sitting around and accusing each other. Cheap revelations that finally emerge from time and darkness. The inability to communicate. All shit."

"They're getting produced, winning prizes."

He removed a card from his wallet. "This has my private telephone number. If you've got a play, call me. If you've got an idea, call me. I think we could work together."

I accepted the card.

"I've got to catch a plane back to the coast. Call me, for Christ's sake, before I have to read another sniveler."

SEVEN

I went out the front door and down the flagstone walk to the water. The waves had left debris scattered along the narrow sand beach, clots of lake weed, snail and clam shells, a bloated carp, the sodden carcass of a gull, scoured pieces of wood. The sand was whorled and ridged. Onrushing green waves rattled the pier's planks in rapid succession, from the end of the pier to where I stood, and the wind carried a fine mist. The two boats wildly pitched and yawed. It was noisy here, with the clattering pier planks and the crashing waves and the howl of the wind in the big oaks.

I walked west along the beach to a fringe of woods, turned, and strolled up the lawn. Tree branches clattered overhead. Dead leaves had drifted against the trunks. I passed the tennis court, a gazebo, banks of flowers, withered and wind-shredded now, and crossed the creek on one of the masonry bridges. Ahead—its porch stilted on a hillside—was the caretaker's cottage. It was old, warped, and badly needed paint. To my left was the Dempsey house and, behind it, the garages and coach house. Not far from the garages, obscured by trees and brush, were two small buildings.

Fifty yards up the driveway the caretaker was still attending to the smoldering stump. He was in his middle to late seventies, lean but with wide shoulders and long, bowed arms and a disproportionately small head. He stood next to the charred stump, in the center of a circle of black, smoking grass, and stared down at me. I nodded but he made no corresponding gesture. There was something in his stance and silent staring that conveyed an enormous hostility, implied violence.

I passed over another bridge, diagonally crossed the grounds (the caretaker watching me all the way), and entered the thicket. One of the buildings was a decrepit shed that smelled of wood rot; the other was a stout dark brown cubical structure with a heavy door that was slightly ajar. There were no windows. I went inside, leaving the door wide open for light and air. The floor, walls, and ceiling were covered with lead sheeting. The floors sloped inward from the walls to a large center drain. At first I thought that this strange room might be a butcher's shed, but then I saw rusty tongs hanging from a nail and realized that it was an old icehouse. Many years ago, before electrical refrigeration, blocks of ice were cut from the lake in winter and stored here. The owner would have ice (and a cold room) available well into the summer months.

When I went back outside I saw that a battered old pickup truck had been parked alongside the driveway. A boy was walking toward the shed. He stopped abruptly when I emerged from the icehouse.

"I thought it would be all right," he said.

He was about sixteen, with the lean and famished look common to that age. He stood awkwardly, holding a small cardboard carton with both hands.

"I know this is a bad time, the day John . . ."

He evidently believed that I possessed some authority here. I approached.

"But . . ."

There were dead birds in the carton, two starlings and some sparrows.

"But the birds have to be fed." The boy wore round-lensed

glasses, and it looked as though his mother or a girlfriend had cut his hair.

"My name is Andrew Neville," I said.

"Tom." He was very shy.

"If you don't mind me asking, Tom—what birds are you going to feed?"

"John's falcons."

"Dempsey kept predatory birds?"

"Raptors. Yes, they're"—he gestured with his head—"in there. I helped take care of them. We, John and me, we hunted them together."

"May I see them?"

"If you like."

"How shall I act?"

"Quiet. Move slow; talk soft. You know. Don't stare at them; they don't like that."

The shed smelled of straw and wood rot and bird mute. There was a hushed rustling, a near-silent stirring toward the back wall. Something in the darkness tensed.

The boy struck a match, took a candle stub from a shelf, and lit it; the wick smoked for an instant and then expanded into a sinuous blade of light. Shadows pooled in the room's corners.

"After a bit I'll turn on the electric lights. Their eyes are very sensitive."

We slowly approached the birds.

"The little one's a kestrel—sparrow hawk. The other is a goshawk."

I had seen photographs of both species, but they looked different now in this musty-smelling shed, in the dramatic candlelight, free except for the rawhide creances.

Tom whistled and crooned to the birds.

The kestrel was small, not much bigger than a robin, though the size of her feet and legs, and the hook of her beak, marked her as a raptor. The goshawk was perhaps two feet in length, with a crown, white stripes above the eyes, and a bluish-gray back. Its breast was mottled gray and white; the eyes glowed a bright translucent red.

"What do you think?" Tom asked.

"I'd like to see them hunt."

"Yeah, that's when they're really alive. This way now. Astarte—the peregrine."

He led through a side door into the adjoining room. The same smells, the same spatial dimensions, and the same sense of being in the presence of a fierce, alien creature. Life intuiting life. I thought of it as a reciprocal uncoiling, a mutual opening of the apertures of perception.

Tom, whistling softly, held the candle aloft. The peregrine's eyes collected and concentrated the light; her eyes, not the candle flame, appeared to be the source of illumination. She was a long-winged bird, slimmer than the goshawk but conveying a great sense of power and speed. She was magic.

The boy moved forward, clucking and whistling. The bird continued to stare at me. Her back was hunched, her beak parted. She shifted her weight from one foot to the other and back again. She seemed to fear and hate me.

"If you'll go outside, Mr. Neville . . ."

I waited outside in the wind for a few minutes, and then the boy appeared.

"She was nervous. A stranger."

"Of course."

"What did you think?"

"She's beautiful."

"She's more than half-wild. She's a haggard, you see. She was wild for three or four years before she was captured. That means she can fly and hunt like a free bird. John used to say that she flew the way you'd fly in a dream if you dared, if you were great.

She makes the short-winged hawks look slow and awkward. John intended to hack her back to the wild next spring."

"Maybe that's what you ought to do."

The boy had lost his shyness. "John woke her very carefully," he said. "So carefully. He stayed with her in the shed, in darkness, for twenty hours. She was a wild bird who'd been captured and mistreated when John bought her. She was suicidal, crazy. But John stayed with her and talked to her. They didn't sleep, neither of them, for twenty hours. John was always there. She learned to trust him. And then Astarte accepted food from his hand and it was over, the waking."

"Could we fly her sometime?"

"Would you like that? I sure would like to hunt her. If it's all right with Mrs. Dempsey."

"Give me your phone number."

"That would be great. John has some land out in the country. There's a pond that usually has some ducks on it. We could go there."

"Fine."

"John used to say that there was nothing like hunting Astarte. The bird was tethered to your mind, your will, he said. It was like killing with a thought."

"You liked John quite a lot, didn't you, Tom? And you miss him."

The shyness returned and he looked away and said, "I couldn't feel worse if it was my own father who died."

Most of the guests were preparing to leave when I entered the house. Laddy Rawling saw me and crossed the room.

"I'll give you a call, Andrew."

"Do that."

"We'll go out for a first-rate dinner. At the foundation's expense, naturally."

"Fine, Laddy."

I waited until the small group gathered around the widow dispersed, and then approached her.

"Thank you for inviting me," I said.

She was pale and tired and beautiful in her sorrow.

"Will you wait until the others have gone?" she said. "I want to talk to you."

"All right. Of course."

I sat in one of the window ovals for half an hour, watching the light gradually fail. The blues and greens darkened and turned to gray. Pinpoint lights began appearing in the shadowy hills across the lake. The wind was not blowing as hard now. Perhaps it would die altogether this evening. When the house was silent I got up and walked over to the bar. Most of the food had been eaten. I was making a drink when Mrs. Dempsey returned.

"I wanted you to stay for a moment. Do you mind?"

"Certainly not."

"Shall we sit down?"

"Yes. Would you like a drink?"

"Bring me a glass of wine, please."

We sat in the window bay and looked out at the smoky blue twilight.

"I wanted to talk to you because I sense that there is a terrible grief in you."

"No."

"I believe I see grief."

"I feel no grief. I'm sorry. I want to be truthful."

"Why did you attend the funeral?"

"I'm not sure, really."

"Why did you take the handkerchief from John's pocket?"

I was silent.

"Perhaps I am wrong."

"I think so."

"Or perhaps your pain is so deep and complex that you are not even aware of it."

"I can't affirm or deny an unconscious guilt."

"I didn't say guilt."

"Pain, I meant."

"I may sound like a sorceress, but grief is what I sensed and still sense. I felt it in the cemetery. That's why I stared at you, because of your pain and because—do you know?—you remind me of John. Yes, you even look a little like him."

"I don't think there's a resemblance."

"Yes, a little. And you move like him, you hold your head a certain way, and your eyes . . . I don't know. It's like you were brothers long separated. Of course, you are a very somber man. John was light; you are . . . heavy. Do you mind me saying that?"

"I knew him for about one year, a long time ago. We weren't especially close. I suppose it's possible that after seeing him at the funeral home's chapel and attending the burial I've been unconsciously imitating certain of his habits and gestures, those that I remember. It could be. The dead sort of occupy us, possess us, for a while. Maybe that's what you see."

"Maybe," she said dubiously.

"I liked and admired John. We all did. He was a rather dashing character back then."

She smiled faintly. "He remained a rather dashing character." A tiny crescent scar at the corner of her mouth dimpled when she smiled.

She said, "Tell me about John when you knew him."

"Well, it's very hard to describe a man, isn't it? Adjectives. He was cheerful, funny, tough, generous, reckless, horny, skeptical."

"And what were you like at that age?"

I thought for a time and then said, "Different from now."

We were quiet. She still held her empty wineglass. I looked at the fine bones and tendons of her hand and wrist.

"I'm so tired," she said.

"I'll go now."

"What do you think the birds at the cemetery meant?"

"Meant?"

"What did those blackbirds signify?"

"I don't understand."

"You *will* think I'm a sorceress. Don't you think it very strange that those hundreds of blackbirds entered the cemetery at that precise moment? And they behaved so crazily—such a din of whistles and chirps, and fluttering here and there, swirling about as if mourning John or protesting his murder."

"I'm not superstitious," I said.

"Ah, well, we Italians are. We see signs and portents in everything."

"The birds were swarming. At this time of year certain species of birds gather from all over the countryside and flock up for the migration south."

"But why in the cemetery?"

"There are many big trees there, and it's surrounded by corn- and wheat fields."

"Is that really all, do you think?"

"Yes."

"You are not at all interested in magical power?"

"No."

"I think life must be very dull for you without mystery."

"There is enough mystery in my life," I said.

"That's a romantic thing to say. You make me curious."

"I'm curious, too, about John's parents. They seem to be a disagreeable couple."

"Oh, yes, you are right. They are narrow, suspicious, vindictive people. Nothing meets their approval, nothing. They resent everyone and everything."

"They resent you?"

"Me especially. They are cruel people. I am just a dago to

them. A wop slut. They even seem to hate half of Dante, the Italian half. I used to wonder how John, so healthy and natural, so free, could possibly have come out of that family. Why didn't they ruin him? But it seems that they didn't touch him at all."

"Who is Roland Scheiss?"

"Oh, that awful man. Isn't he dreadful? He is a lawyer hired by Mr. and Mrs. Dempsey to find John's murderer. And, I believe, to steal John's estate away from me."

"Was Laddy Rawling a good friend of John's?"

"When we moved here Laddy came to see us. He's perhaps not a very nice man, but he is charming. Laddy visited us often, and when we went to Chicago we usually stayed with him. He had a scheme of some kind that would require John's money. But he is charming and he amused us, and John said he liked a man to have at least a little pirate in him."

"Laddy does. And who is Josh?"

"I wanted you to stay so that I could ask you questions. Now you're interrogating me."

"Sorry."

"Josh and the others were John's Los Angeles friends. My friends, too, I suppose. It was kind of them to travel so far. It was awkward. They seemed different here, not very much like the people I thought I knew. All of them are important in television and films."

"You're exhausted. I'll go now."

"Not just yet. I'm afraid to be alone."

"Are you and your son alone in this big house?"

"No. Mary, the girl who takes care of Dante, is here. She's very nice, but she's not intelligent. Does that sound mean?"

"Is Dante all right?"

"How can you tell, at that age? I don't know how much he understands. He may not even remember today when he grows up. But oh, I think it hurts; I think he's been hurt very badly. He hasn't cried yet. He's been stern and angry. And piteous."

She looked away. She did not cry, but she had lost her poise and seemed younger now, and uncertain. Perhaps much of her remarkable composure had been willed. Or maybe she had, in a way, been playing a role in order to maintain control—she was an actress.

"I'm so tired," she said. "Please . . ."

She walked me to the rear door and gave me her hand. "Good night," she said.

"Good night, Claudia."

Halfway between the lake and the city there was a small town called Mill Creek, and tonight as I approached it I saw that the sky above was red and smoky, and a funnel of sparks twisted up toward the stars.

South of town I rounded a curve and saw a great fire burning on the summit of a treeless conical hill. There were cars parked alongside the road and many people—most of them young—swarming excitedly around the area. I parked my car and got out. The little valley trembled with light and shadow. In the interior of the flames I could see the incandesced scaffolding of the pyre. Sparks erupted and swirled away with the smoke. It looked like a volcanic catastrophe.

A mob of screaming youths advanced uphill toward the fire but were halted fifty feet away by the barrier of heat. Some were carrying a figure, an effigy clad in a dark suit and fedora. The effigy appeared to be writhing desperately in their grasp.

It was only a high school's homecoming ceremony. I did not stay to watch the ritual immolation of the effigy.

EIGHT

Cliff Harkey and I stayed late Thursday evening dummying the pages of the magazine.

"Isn't this awful?" Cliff said. "Isn't this humiliating? Christ, a month's work by a dozen people and what have we got? A story about the CEO golfing in Hawaii. A picture of the CEO presenting a check to a charity in Memphis. Here—a bio of the new manager of the Hartford office. Stats, graphs, and, no shit, first-person stories about employees' vacations. And I wanted to be a real writer once."

"So did I, Cliff."

"But you were for a while, sort of."

"Sort of."

"You were almost there. Why did you give it up?"

"I didn't. I've been working on a big project for years."

He grinned at me. "Sure. Aren't we all."

Cliff was a young man whose ambitions far exceeded his talents. He often complained of his bad luck. He wondered why other men got all the breaks. He was beginning to rely on magic now—the racetrack, the state lottery, cheap weekend flights to Las Vegas.

He said, "At least a man ought to be well paid for doing such despicable work. This is sucking the guts out of me, Andrew."

"Right."

"Listen, if the Devil appeared to you tonight and said, 'Andrew Neville, a million human beings, strangers, will die tonight if you wish it, and tomorrow morning you'll receive one tax-free dollar for each and every one of them, buck a head,' would you do it? Say, 'Go for it, old Devil'? Say, 'Spell my name correctly on the check'? Would you do that, Andrew?"

"Would you?"

"Yeah. Oh, yeah, you bet, in an instant. 'Let the appendixes burst, old Devil; set loose the blood clots; let the livers and kidneys fail; let a thousand guns fire and a thousand knives flash.' "

"Let's finish up and get out of here," I said.

On the elevator he said, "Do you want to go up to Wisconsin for the weekend?"

"I don't think so, Cliff."

"My cabin was trashed. You know about my little shack up near Eagle's Nest. Some punks trashed the place, the cop said. It's a mess. I've got to go up there and get it straightened away. We could fish a little, drink beer; hey, maybe a couple of compliant Indian girls would help us out."

"I can't, Cliff. I've got other plans."

"Okay. I've got to drive up there. I thought you might like to come along."

The elevator doors opened; we crossed the nearly deserted lobby and went through the revolving door and onto the sidewalk. We paused.

"How did you hear about the vandalism?" I asked him.

"I said, a cop. A cop came out to my house and told me that my cabin had been trashed."

"A Chicago cop?"

"I suppose. Sure."

"Plainclothes?"

"Yeah, a detective."

"How do you know he was a cop?"

"Come on, Andrew."

"Really. How do you know?"

"He showed me his badge."

I smiled at him.

"He was a cop; you can tell a cop, for Christ's sake. Why would anyone pretend to be a cop just to tell me my cabin has been trashed?"

"What was his name?"

"Smith," he said. Then, "Oh, come on, there are a quadzillion Smiths. Why shouldn't a cop be named Smith?"

"Why should a Chicago cop come to tell you that your cabin in Wisconsin has been vandalized?"

"Because the Wisconsin cops asked him to. Asked the Chicago PD to notify me."

"You really believe that cops have got the time for that kind of Mickey Mouse job?"

"You're paranoid, baby."

It was starting to rain. The lights up and down the street were foggy in the mist. We stepped back into the building's door well.

I said, "What did this cop look like?"

"Well, he looked a lot like that old Russian premier. Remember old Nikita? That's what my wife said. Said she was waiting the whole time for the cop to take off his shoe and pound it on the kitchen table. We were drinking coffee."

"Take your wife to Wisconsin. She can help you clean the cabin."

"I was looking for adventure. Wives kill adventure."

"Well, I've got to get going."

"The cop asked about you."

"He specifically asked about me?"

"No. He was interested—I told him that I had offered the cabin to my friends to use anytime. You remember. He wanted the names of the people I'd given permission to use the place. Your name came up. He asked about you."

"Did he suspect me of trashing your cabin, Cliff?"

He stared out at the gleaming street. "It's funny, isn't it?"

"Hilarious."

"What's going on, Andrew?"

"I couldn't guess."

"I let the guy into my house. I thought he was a cop. I gave him coffee and a piece of cake."

On the way home I stopped at a video rental store. They had a volume that in capsule reviewed nearly all of the movies that had been transferred to videotape. The films were indexed by title, by director, and by the featured actors. Claudia Caporali had five listings: three Italian movies, one British, and one American production.

The store had just one of them in stock, *La Notte Oscura.* I rented it and asked the clerk to order the other four.

It was raining harder now. The city always stank in the early period of a rain: soot, dirt, garbage, smoke. Later the streets would smell fresh.

I parked my car outside the condo building and walked four blocks to a small neighborhood restaurant-bar called *Kelly's Pub.*

I paused in the archway between the dining room and lounge. Roland Scheiss was sitting at the far end of the bar. His face was turned toward the television mounted on the back wall. Two sweaty black heavyweights stalked each other around the ring. I recognized Scheiss by his rounded bulk and the thistlelike sprouts of hair scattered over his round bald head. His small ears, also round, stuck out at right angles. He was an ugly man, an unforgettable man.

I went back out into the rain and searched the streets until I found Scheiss's car, the Buick he had driven on the day of the funeral. Rain beaded on the waxed paint. When the street was clear of traffic I leaned down, removed the valve caps, and let the air hiss out of the two curbside tires. The car listed nicely to port.

I returned to the bar and sat on the stool next to Roland Scheiss. He smelled of Old Spice aftershave and wet wool and cheap cigars. A chewed cigar stub smoldered in an ashtray. He stared at the boxing match on television.

"How are you doing, Roland?" I said.

He turned quickly and for an instant I saw confusion, maybe fear, in his expression, but he recovered and said, "Well, if it ain't my old pal. Buy you a drink, Andrew?"

"Sure."

"Doctor," Scheiss called to the bartender, "Andrew here wants a . . . what do you drink, Andrew?"

"Earl knows."

"Give it to him, Dr. Earl."

"Thanks," I said to Scheiss when the bartender brought me a scotch. "But you go ahead and watch the fight."

"Naw, just a couple of fat coons."

"Have you been waiting for me long?"

"I heard you come in pretty regular."

"You could always phone if you want to talk to me, Scheiss."

"No hurry. This is only the second night I been waiting. I get expenses." His cigar had gone out. He picked it up, placed it between his teeth, and grinned at me.

"I can't believe you're a lawyer."

"Why? Because lawyers take a bath every day? Lawyers got class?"

"No."

"Lawyers got brains?"

I shook my head.

"Lawyers . . . what?"

"Lawyers know how to intimidate in a subtle, safe way. That's what you attend law school to learn—clean intimidation. But you, Scheiss . . . Mentally, you're still a cop. You use dirty intimidation."

He grinned around the dead cigar clenched between his teeth, lifted his chubby palms, and said, "Hey, Andrew, what you got to be intimidated about? Relax, pal."

On the TV behind Scheiss I saw one of the heavyweights knock down his opponent with a series of clumsy but powerful left-right, left-right blows. The man hit the canvas on his back, his head snapping, and then he shivered convulsively for a moment before becoming still.

I called the bartender over and ordered a pastrami sandwich to go. Then I turned to Scheiss and said, "I'm leaving when I finish the drink."

"Don't hurry. Hey, drink; I got an expense account."

"The man is hurt," I said, nodding toward the TV.

"That Claudia is prime loin, don't you think? Prime loin, Andrew."

His little green eyes with their pinpoint irises were intent, watching for my reaction, my anger.

"You like being obnoxious, don't you, Scheiss?" I said.

He grinned.

"I mean, you *enjoy* offending people, disgusting them."

He grinned.

"Maybe you think your foulness is a device, a way of provoking a reaction that might tell you something—but you like it. You like the foulness for its own sake, and you enjoy being despised. You *want* to be odious. And that's who you are."

"Jesus, pal, take it easy. What did I do? You're all nerves this evening, Andrew."

A crowd had gathered around the fallen man in the boxing ring. The television camera focused on a man kneeling by the boxer's side, a doctor, but you couldn't see exactly what he was doing. He might have been preparing an injection.

"I was only kidding about that prime loin stuff, Andrew. Just joking you because you got to stay with her after all of us went away. The night of the burial. Stay with Claudia. Alone in that big house. Christ, that really is prime—I won't say it, Andrew. It's all right. She's a beautiful woman. Is that okay? She's a very sexy woman. Is it all right to say 'sexy,' pal? I'm a dirty cop, I know, a sleazy lawyer. I'm foul and odious. But I wonder—did you fuck her that night, Andrew? And if you did, was it the first time? Or have you been fucking her for a while and no one knows, no one guesses, except for a certain foul and odious individual? Hey, don't worry; you can trust me. Don't get mad. Don't hit me. I'm just jealous. All the time I got a stiff for the lady. But, Andrew, you oughtn't of killed Dempsey. No, no, no, not even for that luscious pussy and not for the money and not—are you listening to me, Andrew?"

On the television I saw some men enter the ring with a stretcher. "He hasn't moved for nearly four minutes," the announcer said. The boxer was a big man, and the paramedics had a difficult time lifting him onto the stretcher. There was an IV tube in the boxer's arm. His opponent and his opponent's handlers were still celebrating the victory.

The bartender brought my pastrami sandwich in a Styrofoam box. I finished my drink and stood up.

"Good night, Roland."

"Hey, wait; don't go, not when we're finally starting to be friends."

It was raining harder now. Pellets of rain jumped off the sidewalk. The gutters were filled with rushing water. Neons and car lights and streetlamps were blurrily reflected on the rain-wet pavement. The low clouds held a dirty pinkish glow.

NINE

At home I hooked up the VCR and inserted the *La Notte Oscura* cassette. I ate the pastrami sandwich with a bottle of beer.

Claudia played the mistress of a Milan industrialist whose son had been kidnapped by a terrorist gang. She had been twenty or twenty-one at the time of the filming, and her beauty was soft, not yet completed. They had lightened her hair and applied too much makeup, so that in the early scenes she looked like numberless starlets and beauty queens. There was nothing exceptional about her. She was gorgeous and vacant. And her acting seemed no more than competent. But in one brief scene the camera penetrated the cosmetic mask and the mask of the character she played and I saw Claudia. Her beauty became individual and human for ten seconds. There was intelligence in her eyes, and mischief. Then the camera changed angles and killed her.

Late in the film there was a seminude scene. Claudia peeled back the sheet and left her lover's bed. She wore only a pair of sheer bikini panties. Her hair was tangled, her makeup gone. Her mouth looked bruised and sad. She walked barefoot to the French doors and stared out into the garden. The camera switched to an exterior shot, and we saw her standing full-length in front of the rain-smeared glass. I stopped the tape there. I halted her movement; I isolated her in that other time and place. I spied on that young Claudia, but not pruriently. The rain-lensed glass blurred her body, abstracted it. I looked at the twenty-year-old Claudia as one might study a lovely impressionist portrait.

The phone rang. It was Scheiss.

"You scum-sucker!" he said. You son of a bitch, I'll get you, Neville, you prick."

I hung up the telephone and returned to the living room. Claudia's pose seemed to have changed slightly during my absence. Her gaze appeared to have shifted so that she gazed more directly into my eyes. There was a sexual challenge in that stare. And there was something provocative in her stance now, too. Perhaps the interruption enabled me to observe another aspect of her. I ran the tape past that scene several more times and then watched the remainder of the movie.

The industrialist, whose son had been murdered by the kidnappers, returned to his wife. The character played by Claudia was bereft beyond consolation, but you did not believe in her sorrow; she was too young and beautiful and lively to suffer long from the defection of that dull, foolish businessman. That girl would not really suffer for another twelve years—until now.

Scheiss telephoned again shortly after midnight. I was watching the movie for the third time.

"Did I mention, Andrew, that your friend Harkey's cabin was vandalized the weekend Dempsey was killed? Did I tell you that? The body was found just a few miles away. Someone must have stayed there. Maybe the same guy who snuffed Dempsey. What do you think, Andrew?"

"I think the state bar will be interested in hearing that you've impersonated a police officer. They'll lift your ticket."

"Hey, Andrew, you wouldn't rat me out of my profession, would you? We're pals. Ain't we pals anymore?"

I fell asleep on the sofa during the third running of *La Notte Oscura*. My dreams were jumbled, incoherent, but I know that Claudia appeared in them, naked and weeping, and John Dempsey was present but invisible, a kind of magnetic force-field—furiously swarming molecules.

TEN

I was sitting in my office Friday morning when I began to tremble. Too much coffee, I thought, too little sleep. But the trembling gradually increased until it became so violent that I could not use a pencil or operate the telephone. I was sweating, a greasy, sour sweat that wet my hair and soaked my shirt. Even breathing was difficult; I could not get enough air. My teeth chattered. My heart leaped wildly. Heart attack, I thought. There was no pain yet, but I shook with a terrible palsy and the oily sweat poured from my body and I could not breathe. Something dreadful had happened or was about to happen. You could not survive this. My vision was distorted, astigmatic. There was not a familiar object in the room. Light shimmered and blurred. Straight lines were refracted as when a stick is inserted in water. The window on the back wall was an opaque block of ice. Surely I was dying. And I thought, *I can't die now, not now.*

My panic vanished gradually, like a long snake entering its hole. Within ten minutes I was able to take a clean sheet of paper from a desk drawer, uncap and fill my fountain pen, and draft a letter of resignation.

The panic returned briefly on the ride down on the claustral elevator, and then I was through the lobby and outside in the sunlight.

★ ★ ★

I drove up to Wisconsin and rented a motel room at the west end of the lake. The motel was situated on a hill behind the village, and I could look out over the treetops and roofs to the water. The entire lake was visible from this height; it looked smooth and cold and was almost exactly the same metallic blue as the sky. Cloud shadows glided from west to east across the water.

A girl answered the telephone. She told me that Claudia was not at home. I could hear a child crying in the background. No, the girl didn't know exactly when Mrs. Dempsey would return—perhaps late in the afternoon?

I walked the two miles down to the lakefront. Some men on a barge were dismantling one of the piers. There were half-tame ducks in the water and gulls scavenging along the pebbled shoreline. The sun was warm and there was not much wind. I went into a bar and ordered two cans of beer and an Italian beef sandwich to go.

"How is the fishing?" I asked.

The bartender said that it was pretty good. Fishermen were taking some Northerns in about thirty feet of water, along the fringe of the weed beds.

I went out on a pier and rented a skiff with an outboard engine, some fishing gear and bait, and for two dollars bought a chart of the lake from an old man who smelled like spoiled fish. There was dried blood and silvery fish scales on his baggy trousers. The old man said a lot of boring things that were intended to be humorous.

The engine smoked, and it clanked loudly when I shifted from reverse to forward. "That motor farts a bit," the old man said.

I tacked through the moored power- and sailboats. The water was very clear; I could see objects ten feet below, fifteen feet, twenty, and then the bottom steeply shelved and the water changed color and turned opaque.

When I passed beyond the keg buoys I increased speed and pointed the skiff down the center of the lake. The water was blue at a distance, but if I looked over the side it became a rich dark green, jade, and glowed with captured sunlight. The chart indicated that the depth here was sixty feet. The far shore lay at the end of a dogleg twelve miles ahead. The shores to my left and right were each about a half-mile away and widening. All around, the hills were mottled with fall colors, and puffs of blue smoke uncoiled here and there among the trees.

I saw big stone or frame houses (and one of marble) set back among the trees. A few were enormous, the size of country hotels. Summer "cottages" of the Chicago rich. And there were crooked masonry fences and canopied piers and lawns as long and broad as a football field. Most of the houses were closed for the winter and the white piers stacked alongshore like dinosaur bones. Caretakers burned dead leaves on the lawns.

There was a town at the east end of the lake. I circled the bay and headed back. It was cooler now. The sun's angle was more acute. After a few miles the skiff passed through the narrows, and far ahead I could see Claudia's house and pier. The water was a darker blue in the late afternoon, exhaling coolness, and I sensed a blackness, a cold dark emptiness, below. The chart informed me that I was passing over the deepest part of the lake, 140 feet.

I anchored about fifty yards offshore, close enough to see squirrels on the lawn and a face behind an upstairs window. Claudia? The boy? The servant girl?

I got out the fishing rod, tied on a hook and baited it with a chub, and began unreeling the line. I could clearly see the chub as it descended. It pulled against the line, twitching the tip of rod, and flashed belly-white just before vanishing into the darkness.

The face was gone from the window when I turned back to the house.

The cold Italian beef sandwich was very good. It came with

a bag of potato chips and some hot green peppers. I ate it with a can of beer and then looked again toward the house. A light had gone on in the big downstairs room, but I saw no one behind the windows. It was very quiet. My hands were cold. I had washed them in the lake after eating, and now they were numb. The bright tree leaves shuddered kaleidoscopically in the breeze. Was I watching or being watched?

The chub was gone from the hook when I reeled in the line; only a worm of viscera remained. I raised the anchor, started the engine, and headed west toward the sunset.

"Claudia?" I said.

"Yes. Who is this?"

It was crazy; I couldn't remember my name.

"Claudia . . . ?"

"Who is this, please? What do you want?"

"Andrew Neville," I said. Do you remember me?"

"Yes, of course."

"I found some old photographs. Of John. Of John and me and Laddy and some others, when we were with the old theater group. Would you like to see them?"

"Oh, yes. Certainly."

"John appears in six or seven of the pictures."

"Yes, I would like to see them. Very much."

"Shall we meet somewhere or shall I come to your house?"

"Where are you?"

"I'm here at the lake, not far from you."

"Well, yes. Why don't you come over?"

"All right. What time?"

"Now? Now is fine."

"I'll be there in fifteen minutes."

I lay back on the bed and closed my eyes. I continued to hear her voice, the precise timbre and rhythm and accent. She had a charming accent. Her voice was altered by the telephone, altered less by the videotape, but it remained true to *the* voice, the voice of Claudia.

She did not cry when she looked at the photographs, but I could tell that she wanted to cry, would have cried if she had been alone.

"He's so young," she said. "He's a baby."

"He was twenty-one there, twenty-two."

"A boy. And in this picture, his smile. Oh, that smile breaks my heart."

"That was his cynical tough-guy smile."

"Tough guy, no. You don't understand."

"I mean that that was his style back then. A tough Irish kid. He liked fighting. He fought in the Golden Gloves that year."

"May I keep this picture, Andrew? Would you give it to me?"

"Of course. You may keep all of them. And I'll have some prints made from the negatives. Five-by-sevens or bigger."

"Thank you."

We sat side by side on a sofa in the big room. The photos were spread out on the coffee table. Claudia wore jeans, sandals, and a gray-blue cashmere sweater. Her long hair was free. She seemed very fragile tonight, physically and emotionally, invaded by grief and despair.

"Claudia," I said. "Maybe you could advise me."

She turned away from the photographs and looked at me. Her eyes and pale skin shone feverishly.

"I've quit my job. I'm putting my apartment up for sale. I'm going to finish my play, and I thought that I might rent a place here on the lake. Maybe you know of a cottage for rent or a real estate agent who might be able to help me."

She was silent for a time, staring at me, and then she said, "The boathouse."

"Pardon?"

"It's small, and it needs work. John used it for a study before he had the rooms above the garage renovated. You could live there. You wouldn't have to pay rent. It *is* small, though."

"Thank you, but I wouldn't want to be an annoyance."

"No, no. You see—I'm frightened to stay alone here. I mean me and Dante and the girl. We're alone. This is a remote place, and it gets so dark at night, and I hear noises. I have difficulty sleeping."

"Well . . ."

"Please. You would be doing me a great favor. To have a man nearby, a friend of John's, would be a relief."

"What about the caretaker?"

"Him! I'll tell you, Andrew, he is one of the things that frighten me. Mr. Stoughton is a very strange man, half-crazy, I think, an angry man. He is always in a quiet rage. And he prowls the grounds at night. I think he stares in through the windows."

"You should fire him."

"Yes, perhaps I shall. Yes. But, you see, he sort of came with this place. He was caretaker for the previous owners for thirty years. They didn't give him a pension. John felt sorry for the man and kept him on. And now I'm afraid."

"Maybe the boathouse would work out well for the both of us."

"I'll give you the key. Go look at it. The electricity is still connected, I think. I'll help you fix it up. We'll paint the walls. I'll buy material for new curtains. Go to the boathouse and then come back and tell me you'll stay there."

"All right, Claudia."

"While you're away I'll fix us something to eat. Are you hungry?"

"Yes."

"Good, then. I'll fix us a meal. I am a very good cook; you'll see. I havn't been able to eat for days. Food chokes me. But I think I am hungry tonight."

The boathouse was white with blue trim and round brass-framed windows like portholes. The lower section was used for storage. A stairway led up to a cedar deck cantilevered out over the water.

The room was about thirty feet long and fifteen wide. It smelled of dust and mildew and mice. There was a sofa that converted into a bed, a matching chair, a desk and chair, a few lamp tables, a chest of drawers, and a small TV. In back, separated by a counter with three stools, was a compact kitchen that contained a two-burner stove, a small refrigerator, a microwave, and cupboards and cabinets. The bathroom, a narrow strip the width of the building, was located behind the kitchen.

The place was small but certainly comfortable enough. The light was good. There was a nicely framed view of the lake and the smoky hills on the opposite shore. Some prints for the bare walls, curtains, throw rugs. There was a telephone jack in the corner. Through a side window I could see the big house. Claudia was there, and the boy, Dante.

I had the feeling of at last being close to home, within reach of home after a long and perilous journey. This place, these few acres, vibrated with a profound emotional resonance.

ELEVEN

Dempsey's farm was located nineteen miles northeast of the lake on a gravel back road. It was in a country of smooth low hills sliced into rectangles of crop- and pastureland, with lowland ponds, iron-grid windmills, and canted red-oxide barns. The soil and tree trunks were black in the rain. Black-and-white dairy cows huddled against the sides of barns or beneath wind-undulant trees. Poplars grew along some of the fence lines, and there were scattered woods of oak and maple, their late-autumn colors dulled now in the misty light

Dempsey's farm was similar to others I had seen on the drive, although it appeared less well maintained; the house was vacant, windows boarded over, and both house and barn badly needed paint.

I parked the car and we got out into the muddy yard. It was still raining lightly, but the clouds were starting to break up. Tom carried the hooded falcon on his gloved hand. Her tiny silver bell tinkled as she shifted to maintain balance.

We crossed the yard, passed through a gate in the barbed-wire fence, and started across a large cornfield. Most of the corn had been harvested, though some rows of seven-foot stalks remained along the fence lines and in random strips across the field. Those stalks still bore their heavy ears of corn. The bayonet-shaped leaves were brown and wilted. Tom said that Dempsey had leased his fields to a neighboring farmer. By agreement some of the corn was left standing to provide cover and feed for pheasants.

The falcon, Astarte, rode light on Tom's fist, occasionally spreading her wings to maintain balance.

We passed between the top and middle wires of a fence and started across a pasture. The ground was hard. There were white rocks and disks of cow droppings. The long grass, combed and flattened by the prevailing west wind, was the color of ripe wheat.

The pasture ran fairly level for about seventy yards and then ascended a steep hillside to a woods. The clouds parted and sunlight spectrally burst among the trees, sparking conflagrations of scarlet and rust and gold. We paused there. Sunlight and shadow, the ticking rustle of wind-spun leaves. Great oaks here, and box elder, maple, walnut, chestnut, and ash. Corpse-gray mushrooms sprouted out of rotten logs. A thick, wet compost of leaves lay underfoot.

Tom inserted his index finger into the falcon's breast feathers and gently tickled; the bird opened her beak, exposing the pink, tapered tongue, uttered a faint cry, and fluffed all of her feathers.

"She likes you," I said.

"I guess so."

"She's beautiful."

"During medieval times only the highest nobility could own a peregrine falcon. Kings, princes, dukes. That's what John told me."

I reached out to touch her breast, as Tom had, and she swiftly stabbed downward with her beak and slashed the webbing between my index finger and thumb.

"Bitch!" I said furiously.

"Are you all right?"

The gash was deep and flowing blood.

"It looks bad."

I got out a handkerchief, wadded it, and pressed it between my thumb and index finger. The cloth gradually turned red.

"We'd better go back," Tom said.

"No. I'll get it sewed up later. We'll go ahead and hunt the bitch."

"I'm sorry, Andrew," the boy said. "She's never done anything like that before. And she's wearing the hood—they're usually very passive when hooded."

"Never mind. Let's go."

A muddy path led through a tangled undergrowth of alder and catbrier and black snakeroot and feverwort and maidenhair fern. The handkerchief was soaked with blood now. We went on, circling the thorny thickets, and finally came to a rusty barbed-wire fence. Here the woods ended and another field began, a long, gentle hill covered with wheat stubble. The field leveled out well below and then stretched on to another fence lined with poplars. The field was bound on the west by a road and in the east by a cornfield. Farm buildings were visible in the plains beyond the poplar trees. A shallow creek twisted down the center of the wheat field, lazily submitting to the gradient, and then entered a three- or four-acre pond in the southwest corner. There was an old skiff pulled up on the cracked-mud shore, and a dozen or so mallard ducks paddled near the marshy area along the south bank.

"Your hand is still bleeding," Tom said.

"Forget it. What do you want me to do?"

"Okay. Cross the field well east of the pond, then walk down behind the line of trees. When you come up on the pond the ducks will spook."

"Right."

"Ducks will usually stay down when there's a falcon in the air. They're safe on the water. Astarte will be at her pitch by the time you reach the pond, and she'll attack one of the ducks when they flush."

I passed through the fence and started walking downhill. The wet earth had a sour, decayed smell. It was a humid morning, hot now that the sun had emerged, and here and there the ground smoked with vapor.

There were two rows of poplars, staggered so as to effect a windbreak, and I walked down the aisle between the trees. There was a chill aqueous light here and a rich golden radiance overhead. The poplar leaves shivered in a breeze so faint that I could not feel it on my cheek.

The pond had a stagnant smell, and when I came closer I saw that most of it was scummed with algae. The ducks were gone. A turtle carcass rotted on shore.

I looked up: the falcon, leather jesses trailing, bell chiming faintly, was swiftly beating upward in a helical ascent. When she was about one hundred and fifty feet above the ground she emitted a thin, shrill cry that sounded more mournful than fierce. I saw that her wingtips were curved upward at the tips, bent by the weight of the air, and her dark eyes saw me, saw the ducks, saw everything.

Tom, still on the hilltop, pointed toward the marshy area. Evidently the ducks had taken refuge among the cattails and saw grass.

Excited, without thinking, I ran into the marsh. I splashed through shallow pools, shouting, stumbled through crackling cattails. I sank ankle-deep into the stinking mud. Then I nearly stepped on a duck that scrambled deeper into the grass; then I was startled by a soft huffing explosion, like gasoline igniting, and half a dozen ducks rose steeply out of the marsh and planed low over the pond. Three settled on the water, a fourth circled and returned to the marsh, and two more—a drake and a hen—flew hard and low toward the wheat field. They were no more than twenty feet above the ground.

The falcon seemed to stall in the air, twist convulsively, and then she dived. She beat her wings furiously for fifteen or twenty strokes and then half-folded them back. Her body appeared elongated. It happened too quickly for me to isolate the action into its separate details. But the two birds converged at great speed, and there was the sound of impact, and a puff of feathers. The drake, his body slack now, his momentum carrying him forward as he fell, struck the ground about thirty yards beyond the pond.

Astarte angled upward, climbed to sixty feet, uttered another cry, and then settled down upon her prey. She mantled over the duck, shading him with her wings, lowered her head, and plucked some breast feathers.

Tom, grinning, was walking down the hill. He raised a hand, the thumb and index fingers formed into a circle, and shouted something that I couldn't understand.

I waded out of the marsh and sat on the bank. The falcon had been beautiful and terrible. At first I had pitied the ducks, hoped that they might escape, but then at some point I had sort of become the falcon, saw through her eyes, felt her urgency, shared her need. Astarte. She was swift, pure, deadly.

When Tom was about twenty feet away from the falcon he dropped to his knees and slowly shuffled forward, crooning and whistling. He carried a piece of raw meat. The falcon bristled. She crouched over the duck and stared at the boy.

Tom had previously explained it: He would "make up" slowly, tempt her off her kill with the raw meat, gather in the jesses, and slip on the plumed hood. Hooded again, she would become docile; the flame would burn lower, cooler; she would partially die until the next time.

I lay back on the ground and closed my eyes. The sun was warm. Retinal flashes, a plunging dark object that might have been an afterimage of the falcon. I had ruined a good pair of shoes in the water. My lacerated hand throbbed. I inhaled the odors of the grasses and the sour stink of the pond. Astarte. Dempsey's bird, now mine. I intended to seduce her, master her, seize her. She is mine.

Dante—a pretty, cheerful faun—was playing in the gazebo when we returned. He was excited by the falcon and her kill. Tom let him stroke the mallard's iridescent neck feathers. The child crooned softly, his eyes half-closed, his lips pursed. "Oh," he murmured. "Oh."

He looked at me. "Is he dead?"

"Yes," I said.

"The bird is dead," he said softly, to himself. And then his expression changed, compressed and wrinkled, and he began crying.

PART II

ICE

TWELVE

Early the next morning I rented a small tow trailer and moved some of my things up to the boathouse. Everything else would go into storage. A real estate agent had told me that he expected no difficulty in selling my apartment, at a substantial profit if I were patient.

I drove up to the lake at ten and promptly began scrubbing the boathouse. It had been neglected. The little oven and two-burner stove were filthy, there were cobwebs everywhere, and mice scratched and scrabbled inside the walls. I moved the furniture out onto the redwood deck and left the doors and windows open while I worked. I scrubbed everything down, vacuumed the floor, polished the round bronze window frames, and repaired a leaky faucet.

At two o'clock I went out onto the deck and sat in the sun. The lake had a smooth enameled gloss. There was a fishing skiff anchored down near the point, and across the lake a sailboat was trying, without much success, to tack into a nearly nonexistent breeze. Smoke from leaf fires clouded the hills beyond. It was quiet and very pleasant here, neither too warm nor too cool, autumnal. The trees were in prime color now.

Tomorrow, I thought, I'll paint the walls. Paint the outside, too, maybe—why not? Clean the soot deposits out of the potbellied wood stove and its chimney pipe. And later in the week it might be worthwhile to tear up the carpet; I suspected that a fine hardwood floor might be concealed beneath that rag.

It was good to sit in the lemony sunlight and think of the tasks ahead, the work to be done in preparation for winter. The boathouse could be made into a cozy little lair, refuge from the cold, refuge from my past. Perhaps I could write a new play here. Why not, since I felt renewed and life again possessed meaning (although that meaning was not yet clear to me). I realized that I had been depressed for years, ill, half-paralyzed by despair. Strangely, killing Dempsey had restored hope. His death was my resurrection.

"Andrew? Hello."

I stood and saw Claudia coming toward me down the brushy shore path. She carried a wicker picnic basket and a Thermos jug. She wore jeans, a sweater, and a paisley scarf over her hair.

I said her name, "Claudia." And again: "Claudia."

She paused at the bottom of the steps. "I saw your car."

"Yes. I didn't want to disturb you."

"You probably don't have anything to eat. I brought you food."

"Thank you."

She climbed the stairs and gave me the basket and vacuum flask. "Is everything all right?"

"It's wonderful."

"Do you have electricity?"

"Yes."

"I'll call the phone company if you like."

"Yes, please."

Claudia still appeared tired, listless. She wore no makeup. She looked slender, thin even, in a dress, but the jeans and sweater emphasized her female roundness, the soft curves of breast, waist, hip, and thigh. She removed the scarf and freed her smoky dark hair.

"Sit down," I said.

"Yes, all right. For a minute."

She sat on the easy chair I had dragged out of the boathouse; I leaned back against the deck railing. Sunlight glazed her hair, flecked her eyes with commas of light. Her skin, except for the little crescent scar, was flawless even in this hard autumnal glare.

"I brought you two sandwiches. Ham. Do you like ham?"

"Yes."

"And black coffee."

"I'll get two cups. You'll have coffee with me, won't you?"

"Yes. And then I must go."

I returned from the kitchen with two coffee mugs, filled them, and sat across from her.

"Well," I said.

"It's all right, isn't it?"

"What?"

"This—the boathouse."

"Oh yes, it's fine. I like it very much. Very."

"Good."

She took a cigarette from a package that lay on the coffee table and leaned forward as I lit it. She smoked quickly, nervously, but without inhaling.

"Claudia."

She met my gaze for a moment and then glanced away.

"How are you doing?"

She shrugged.

"If you need to talk . . ."

"It's hard," she said. "It's very, very hard."

"Yes."

"If it weren't for my son . . . I don't know."

"Yes."

"I loved John so much. You know, until I met him, I didn't think that I was capable of that total love. I didn't really believe there was such a thing. No, I didn't want to give myself up that way. I knew the danger."

"It's dangerous, yes," I said.

"But I have Dante. John lives in Dante, doesn't he?"

"Of course he does."

"Still, you can't lie to yourself; John is gone."

"Yes."

"Dead."

"I'm sorry, Claudia."

"Dead. Well, what is there to say? John is dead."

"Time," I said. "It's such an awfully trite thing to say—but time heals, Claudia."

"I suppose. Usually, yes. But that healing—isn't that a betrayal?"

"I don't know."

"Forgive me. I shouldn't inflict my suffering on you. It's ugly."

"You must talk to someone."

"No, I must not."

"If you talk to anyone, talk to me."

"Why you?"

"Because I understand."

"Do you?"

"Yes."

"Do you really?"

"I do."

"Perhaps so," she said, rising. "I told you that I sensed that you felt very deeply about John's death. You denied it. But perhaps you are like me, with me, in this?"

"Yes."

When she was gone I poured another mug of coffee. My hand was steady. Was I insane? I thought, without emotion or conviction, that I had to be odious, a monster, to continue in my deception—the murderer soothing the victim's widow. The compassionate killer. Still, I would not bring John Dempsey back to life if I could. I'd kill him again now, and twice more tomorrow.

THIRTEEN

The weather continued clear for a week, chilly at night, sunny and warm during the daylight hours. Sometimes the lawn was white with frost when I awakened, and wisps of vapor arose from the lake. Acorns and black walnuts fell from the big trees. The leaves lost color, turned brown and crisp, and rocked gently to earth. Each afternoon the caretaker raked the leaves into piles and burned them. The air, night and day, was faintly hazed with smoke.

Workmen arrived to take the boats away to winter storage, and later they returned to dismantle the pier and stack it onshore.

The lake changed color according to the light; its various hues reminded me of the names of gemstones—amethyst, lapis lazuli, sapphire, aquamarine . . . At night the water was usually a glassy indigo speckled with starlight.

Early one morning I was gathering walnuts from the lawn when the caretaker appeared on his rickety front porch and shouted down to me. I couldn't understand his words, so I just waved and went on picking up walnuts and dropping them into a burlap sack. Mr. Stoughton hurried down the porch steps and down the lawn toward me. There was anger in his walk, in his posture and expression.

"Them's *my* nuts," he said hoarsely.

"All of them?"

"I collect them. I always collect them."

I said, "I think there are enough walnuts for you, me, and the squirrels."

"They *mine,* goddamn it!"

It was ridiculous: he was seventy-some years old and prepared to fight me over a bag of walnuts. His hands were clenched into fists. His long, bony face was distorted by rage. I thought that he might attack me, or might instead suddenly weep.

"They mine," he said. "Give them me," and he held his hand out toward my sack, but he did not advance.

The man was unbalanced, and normally I would have conceded the walnuts to him, but Claudia gave in to him all the time and Dante feared the old man; he was a tyrant and becoming more tyrannical every day.

"Give them me," he said again.

"I'm keeping them. And I'm going to get another ten sacks and collect every nut on the property, excluding you. What do you think of that, Stoughton?"

His eyes bulged. There were flecks of saliva at the corners of his mouth. "You're a crazy man," he said. "You watch; I'll get you, crazy man. Just you watch." He turned abruptly and stalked up the lawn in his forward-leaning gait, turned to glare at me when he reached his house, then went on up the porch steps and through the front door.

When my sack was filled I took it to the boathouse and spread the walnuts out on the deck. The green husks had a lemony scent. When the sun dried and blackened the husks, the nuts would be ready to eat.

Later I circled through the brush patch behind the boathouse and looked out at the lawn. Mr. Stoughton had a wire rake and was dragging the walnuts into piles. It didn't look as though he intended to leave any for the squirrels.

Dempsey had fitted out a study upstairs in the old coach house. Claudia gave me a key and asked me to look for certain papers required by the lawyers. She could not bear to visit Dempsey's study, sort through his possessions.

An outside stairway led up to what had once been the coachman's—and later a chauffeur's—living quarters. The partitions had been removed, and it was all one big room now, with polished oak floors, age-blackened ceiling beams, and a spaced row of sash windows extending along the east wall. The rear half of the room was carpeted and the walls paneled in walnut. And there was a huge oak desk with a leather-upholstered swivel chair, a smaller desk set at a right angle that contained a computer keyboard and screen, three stacks of old wooden cabinets, a television-stereo-VCR console, a leather sofa and three leather chairs, and a liquor cabinet with a small built-in refrigerator. A roll-up movie screen was situated high on the front wall, and I found a .35 mm movie projector and cartons of film reels in a closet.

Dempsey had not stinted in fashioning his study. It was suitable for a Hollywood writer-producer, fit for a mogul.

The place was cool and musty-smelling. I turned the thermostat up to seventy degrees, sat behind the desk, picked up the telephone, and heard a dial tone. "Send in a naked starlet," I said.

A door behind the desk opened into a bathroom. I washed my hands with lavender-scented soap and examined my face in the mirror. *You devil.* Perhaps I ought to grow a beard or mustache as an assertion of change.

I returned to the big room and inventoried the contents of the file cabinets. Dempsey had been very orderly. That surprised me; then I realized that of course a man of his wealth employed orderly men—lawyers and accountants and investment counselors.

Financial documents filled two drawers: insurance policies; stock and bond certificates; tax returns; bank accounts; mortgage papers on this property, the farm, and a house in Malibu; semi-annual statements on his television and movie residuals; papers concerning properties like boats and automobiles; papers establishing the provenance of artworks, including a Derain and two Hockneys; bills paid and bills due; debits and credits. Some very rough calculations informed me that Dempsey's estate might be worth around $6 million, give or take a million.

Claudia had neglected to give me the combination to the safe. Tomorrow, then. And perhaps tomorrow I would inventory his video and film library; no doubt all of Claudia's TV and movie appearances would be in the collection. And it might be interesting to see what I could bring up on his personal computer.

I poured some forty-year-old cognac into a snifter and lit one of Dempsey's Honduran cigars.

This is very nice, John.

There were half a dozen crows in the little cemetery, and when the sentry, high in a big oak, cawed a warning they all lifted and beat away toward a sere cornfield. As we passed through the skewed iron gate, I recalled the judgmental crows on the day I'd killed Dempsey. The collective noun for a flock of crows was *murder.* A pack of dogs, a gaggle of geese, a murder of crows. Claudia was startled by the birds, halted for an instant, then went on.

"They are still here," she said.

"No, I think those were grackles last time."

We walked slowly so that Dante would have no difficulty in keeping up. It had rained during the night, and the cemetery was sodden, hushed, and mossy. Lichens grew on the older gravestones. The ground was covered ankle-deep with wet leaves. There were still leaves on the trees, but they had lost all color, were brown and shriveled.

We could not find Dempsey's grave for a time and wandered lost among the aisles and stones and the few pretentious monuments and statues.

"There it is."

"No, it's over there."

Dante, head down, kicked his feet through the drifted leaves. We could still hear the distant harsh cawing of the crows. A dispute of crows; an insolence of crows; a murder of crows. The sun shone brightly for a moment and then was reabsorbed by clouds.

John Thomas Dempsey
"The virtuous man honors
both himself and God."

The black granite headstone was so highly polished that it reflected the ground and trees. A wreath of leafy vines—grape? laurel?—had been chiseled around the perimeter. The grave mound itself was buried beneath a blanket of sodden leaves.

"Do you think it's all right?" Claudia asked.

"Yes." What did it matter? "The quote is from . . . ?"

"Dante."

The boy looked up at the sound of his name.

Claudia smiled at him. "Another Dante," she said. A poet."

The boy stared at his mother, trying to gauge her mood, emotion, and so consequently determine what he should feel.

Dante—crisp black hair and eyebrows, shining dark eyes, pink lips, and a pink blush on his cheeks. A cherub.

"Ah," Claudia said softly.

The three of us were seized by the same thought: down there, a couple of yards beneath us, lay Dempsey—husband, father, victim. I could clearly imagine the corpse lying supine on white silk, suit jacket buttoned, tie knotted, hands folded over his breast. Disemboweled, exsanguinated, embalmed, the terrible knife wounds neatly sutured. And then the image changed: the eyes were open now, seeing; the mouth curved in the ironic Dempsey half-smile; the mind awakened.

Claudia wept silently. Dante critically watched her and then he, too, started crying.

We placed flowers at the head of the grave, backed away, turned, and walked to the car.

FOURTEEN

"Hello?"

"Hello, Andrew."

"How did you get my number, Scheiss?"

"I asked directory assistance."

"It's an unlisted number."

"Then I must of got it some other way. Settling comfortably into your new quarters, Andrew? Close to the lake, close to the widow lady. You gonna invite me to the boathouse warming, pal?"

"Sure."

"On second thought, never mind. It'd prolly be an effete affair. Chardonnay, Brie, tiny sandwiches with the crusts cut off."

"For you, Scheiss, I'll have a bucket of swine offal."

"Not nice. Why are you so mean to me, Andrew?"

"Because you're a filthy rodent."

"Oh, that."

"Because you're rotten, corrupt clear through."

"Oh, well, that. Nobody's perfect. Not even Andrew Neville. You sneaking murdering shit, you butcher. Hack and slice a man to pieces and then talk holy about rodents and corrupt. Oh, yeah, chum, morally superior while you snuff the husband and sniff the lady."

"I can't imagine why the world has let you live this long, Scheiss."

"I don't turn my back on the killer scum of this world like Dempsey made the mistake of doing. That's why. That's how I'm still around to telephone my good friend Andrew and have a friendly and productive chat."

"Get to the point."

"No point. I just decided to reach out and touch someone."

"Touch for how much?"

"That's good. That's funny, kid. Listen, I been talking to people in your neighborhood here, neighbors, bar and restaurant personnel, you know. Making inquiries. You got an alibi, but there's holes in it. Holes the DA can drive an indictment through. And up there around Eagle's Nest? You were careful, Andrew, but not careful enough I don't think. I'm spinning a sticky web. A web that gets bigger and stickier every day. I'm the spider and you're the fly. That's one thing you ain't called me yet: spider."

"Listen, don't you have to know something about the English language to pass the bar exam?"

"Nah. Not in Illinois. They make it so easy for the niggers and spics that we Rolands squeeze through."

"Have you ever won a case, Roland?"

"My cases don't make it to court. I try to settle them over the telephone, over a drink, over a putt. I'm a negotiator, my friend, a compromiser. You give me this, I grant you that. Quid pro quo. That's Latin. Litigation is a last resort. Sending a prosperous murdering couple to the penitentiary is a last resort. They become a burden to society and what do I get out of it? It's better to compromise, to deal. Do you understand what I'm talking about, Andrew?"

"You're talking about extortion."

"I resent that; I really do. You insist on thinking the worst of your fellow humans."

"But you aren't human."

"See? There you go again."

"Call again the next time you're feeling stupid."

"Wait! Wait, Andrew. One thing. How often do you and the lovely widow do it? Fuck, you know, all that stuff. Man, I can see it, feel it, smell it."

"Roland, if you need a little telephone porn to accompany your self-abuse, dial a 900 number."

"Funny. But seriously, that Claudia is prime loin. I've only seen her a few times, but man! I try to stand real close to her. She's hot. I mean her body temperature is high, maybe she's always running a low-grade fever, but you can feel the heat coming off the woman and smell her like musky, feverish scent. Man! If it was me. If it was me, pal, we'd lie together naked on the bed, me and the widow, not touching, not for a while, just sort of inhaling each other. And then. Jesus, I can hardly bear thinking about it."

"Scheiss, I don't think you understand the danger you're in."

"Fix me up with her. That's part of our deal. I get to spend a whole night with Claudia. Talk to her. Explain that for one night her body is mine. That's the deal, nonnegotiable. Tell her. It won't be so bad. She might like it. I'm ugly, but I got technique. Andrew? Don't hang up. Help me out on this one thing and I'll go easy on the financial aspect."

FIFTEEN

I had killed a decent man; maimed the heart and mind of a fine woman; damaged a child; and yet I felt no remorse, no guilt, did not suffer, slept well, and awakened cheerful. Was I a psychopath? Apparently, but if so, I had not always been one. A new dark self had begun to emerge on the day I'd killed Dempsey.

Each morning I spent three or four hours in Dempsey's study above the garage. It was a comfortable place, private, with a good view and enough material to amuse and occupy me throughout the winter. There was the extensive film library; cassettes of all the television shows that Dempsey had written or produced; file cabinets stacked full with scripts and correspondence; and a Mac computer that yielded a journal of Dempsey's last six months.

The journal had not been concealed: I had simply typed a series of words: "DIARY, NOTES, NOTEBOOK, JOURNAL"—and there it was on the screen.

Dempsey had been a more complex and intelligent man than I'd supposed, formidable in ways, tough and ironical and perceptive. Claudia, too, was revealed as possessing a far richer personality than I had so far observed; grief had dulled her, made her passive, eliminated the emotional extremes that largely delineate human character. It was obvious that they had loved each other very much, though in the journal Dempsey confessed to a brief, insignificant affair with an actress.

Mixed in with the more personal entries were references to

half a dozen persons I didn't know, odd scraps of conversation, psychological insights, and scattered lines that were meaningless when deprived of context. I was astonished to find my own name frequently mentioned. "Don't forget that Neville only appears cold; the coldness is deceptive, like the snow on an active volcano." "Neville is capable of going from placidity to rage and back again without transition." "Character is Fate; but with Neville, Fate is Character."

I skimmed through this electronic journal, pausing to read each mention of this "Neville." In many ways he was like me; in other respects he was my opposite, a sort of reverse döppelganger. Finally it occurred to me that Dempsey had mixed together his personal entries with notes for a writing project, probably a movie script. Writers often used the names of people they knew or had once known and borrowed a trait, a way of speaking, an actual incident, without attempting a full or accurate portrait. So the appearance of this literary Neville was not so large a coincidence as it first seemed. Even so, it was disturbing, like meeting an alternate Andrew Neville, like reading a dead man's prophetic scribbles.

It was likely that the script, partial or complete, was stored in the computer, guarded by a code word or some relevant numerals—birth dates, anniversaries, significant numbers reversed or used without change. Names: Dante, Claudia, John . . . Perhaps there was a clue in the journal. I decided to spend half an hour each morning trying to discover the password.

Dempsey's journal interested me in itself and as a kind of psychological purgative. Maybe I could get to know myself (my new self) as I came to know John Dempsey, Claudia, Dante, and the semifictional Neville. I, too, would write a journal, in narrative form, beginning with my sighting of the deer and the murder and proceeding through to the end (whatever and whenever that end). A confession without any expectation of absolution.

The rift in the fog closed before I could notch an arrow. . . .

Frank Stoughton, the surly caretaker, went to a VA hospital in Milwaukee for a minor operation, the removal of hemorrhoids (which he called "piles"). He was gone three days. On the middle day I walked up to his house and looked around. It was an old frame building that smelled of wood rot. The front and back doors were well secured by conventional locks and padlocks and deadbolts. The sash windows, upstairs and down, were covered by storm glass and wire mesh screens. It was a shabby little fortress. His obvious desire to keep people out challenged me to enter. What was he concealing in there? It amused me to imagine that old Stoughton might be another Wisconsin killer-cannibal like Ed Gein and Jeffrey Dahmer.

Every fortress has its weak point; here it was the narrow garage—the sliding door was secured by only a pair of padlocks. I got a screwdriver from the boathouse, removed the hasps, lifted the door, and entered the cluttered, musty space. Carpentry tools, plumbing tools, lawn and gardening implements, seed, glass jars filled with rusty screws and nails, half-empty buckets of paint, hardened putty, gasoline cans, glass jugs of turpentine, a couple of rusty old lawn mowers, a ten-gallon can of solidified tar, hooks and hinges and hasps and hangers, odd lengths of scrap wood, bales of insulation, greasy motor parts spread out on a workbench, a frozen lathe, a thousand keys . . . There was just barely enough room left for Stoughton's beat-up VW.

A zinc-sheathed door not more than five feet high led from the garage into the basement. It was a heavy door with iron strip hinges and an old iron lockbox. A problem, except that the garage contained Frank's collection of keys: trays and bucket and jars of keys, most of them old and simple, designed to turn the simple tumblers of a nineteenth-century lock. I tried twenty or so keys until finally one withdrew the bolt with a dry click.

The basement ceiling was low; I had to move in a crouch among the piles of debris. The stone walls and concrete floor were black with coal dust. There was an old asbestos-padded furnace with its pipes and gauges, a coal bin now filled with broken furniture, wood boxes, cardboard boxes, a double sink, an old washing machine, a bicycle frame, trunks whose bronze hinges were green with verdigris, boxes, and more boxes.

A steep stairway led to another door. It was closed but not locked. The house itself was neat and clean and severely ordered. A smell of pine-scented disinfectant lingered in the air. The rooms were cubical and small: a kitchen, a dining area that merged into the living room (a screened porch outside), a bathroom whose old porcelain toilet and claw-footed bathtub were iron-stained. A stairway led up to the two upstairs bedrooms, equal in size with a bathroom between, and above—reached through a trapdoor in the ceiling—was a cluttered crawl space that smelled of mildew and dust.

The place was sparsely furnished: iron frame beds, spindly wooden chairs, scarred tables and cabinets, old lamps with greasy parchment shades. There were no photographs anywhere, no mementos of a life, no pictures on the stained wallpaper, no radio or TV or phonograph, no bookshelves, no telephone, nothing but a sterile discomfort. It was as if the house had been abandoned thirty years ago.

Vacant house, vacated soul. But then I discovered a secret room off the kitchen, a narrow, deep, rectangular space that had once been a pantry. The door was blocked by an empty china cabinet that I wrestled aside. Here is where Stoughton hid his private—pathetic—self. The many oilcloth-covered shelves were crowded with his odd booty: objects found and objects stolen, objects no doubt salvaged from dumps and garbage bins, objects as old as the century and as new as last week.

There were keys (more keys!) and polished brass doorknobs, children's toys, stacks of old mail stolen from rural mailboxes, plaster saints and chipped glass figurines, car license plates going back to 1927, several dozen fountain pens, an alpine-style hat with green feathers in the band, tarnished silverware, more old children's toys—an Erector set, Lincoln Logs, Tinkertoys—all carefully sorted and in their original boxes. Hair pins, a curling iron, tiny patent-leather shoes with silver buckles, a cut glass decanter, playing cards, stacks of 45 rpm phonograph records, a music box that played "Stardust" when the lid was opened, dimestore jewelry, a tambourine, cheap pocketwatches, a straight razor, forty-year-old girlie magazines that were hardly salacious by today's standards. And dolls, fifty staring blue-eyed dolls perched coquettishly on the shelves, rag, plaster, porcelain, wood, plastic, and pewter dolls, a few of them of some value to a collector, but most with a fractured limb or mangy hair or an empty eye socket.

My inexpensive point-and-shoot camera, taken from the boathouse deck a week ago, was there; Dante's lead soldiers, left out in the gazebo overnight, were there; Claudia's kidskin driving gloves were there.

The room was a mad confusion, a glance into the cluttered, unhealthy mind of old Frank Stoughton.

Tom continued to attend to the birds after school. He fed them, cleaned the mews, renewed the licenses that permitted us to possess raptors, medicated the kestrel when she became ill, and repaired a broken pinion feather on the falcon. On the weekends we exercised them out on the lawn, flying them to the lure, a piece of meat (stuck with feathers) tied to a long rawhide line that we whirled around and around. You could hear the whistly compression of their wings, closely observe their speed and darting aerial maneuvers. Their fierce eyes glowed.

One day we took Astarte hunting at Dempsey's farm. She was uncontrollable. We thought we had lost her. It took four hours to finally coax her back to Tom's gloved fist.

As we were driving home I said, "Astarte is very spooky around me."

"She's wild. I mean a haggard can be awfully hard to manage."

"Tom, I'd like to take over her care. Feed her, handle her, fly her."

He was silent.

"She doesn't know who her master is."

"I haven't done anything wrong."

"I know that, Tom. I want you to continue taking care of the other birds. Your pay will remain the same. I'll need your help and advice. But I'll be the only one to feed or handle Astarte for a while. Okay?"

"If you say so."

"Good. Now, the holidays are coming up soon. Why don't I give you your Christmas bonus early, now, so that you'll have a little extra cash in your pocket?"

I reached into my breast pocket and removed a 100-dollar bill.

"Take it, Tom. You've earned it."

"Thanks. Thanks a lot."

He was hurt. He had come to think of Astarte as his bird, his alone. I believed that he had unintentionally, probably unconsciously, confused Astarte and set her against me. I couldn't have that. Astarte was mine.

That night I entered the shed and stood quietly in the pulsant darkness. I could not see Astarte, but I sensed her presence. She was hungry, I knew, furious. She moved, a faint rustling of feathers, a click of talons on the stone perch, an exhalation.

I lit a candle and watched as light expanded to fill the room and infiltrate her dark eyes. I whistled softly. I crooned her name. The perch was a flat stone about forty inches long and twenty wide, mounted on a pair of sawhorses. Her jesses were slack enough so that she could move freely around the stone.

I pulled on the leather gauntlet and slowly advanced. The candle flame was duplicated in her eyes. A few more steps. She spread her wings slightly, and her beak parted. I offered her a strip of raw meat. She struck swiftly, like a snake, but at my hand and not the meat.

"Bitch," I said.

She hated me. That was all right; I wanted her obedience, not her affection.

Astarte refused food that night and for two days afterward. At last she consented to snatch a piece of chicken from my gauntleted hand and then, mantling over it, she hissed at me.

"Bitch," I said.

SIXTEEN

"Hello?"

"Bonjour, my friend. Buenos días. Good morning."

"Take a bath, Scheiss. I can smell you over the phone line."

"Is that nice? I thought offensive body odor was something you dare not even tell your best friend about."

"Well, there it is. You stink."

"I'm a carnivore, Andrew. Carnivores smell bad."

"You're not a carnivore; you're a scavenger."

"Yeah, maybe. You got something there, buddy. But the scavenging has got to get better pronto, or you and the widow lady are going to do some hard time."

"Hold on a second. I want to get my tape recorder going."

"Okay."

"Just a second now."

"Sure."

"I'm putting in a clean cassette."

"Fine. Ready yet?"

"Not yet. All right, go."

"You want me to sing something?"

"Speak a little louder, if you don't mind."

"Right. My name is Roland G.-for-Goethe Scheiss, and I am an attorney-at-law in good standing, at last word anyway, with the Illinois Bar and various and sundry professional and social organizations. I got body odor. I am aware that this conversation is being recorded. I enthusiastically acquiesce in the recording of my words at this time. How am I doing?"

"Good. Keep going."

"I have body odor and bad breath from bad teeth. There is as yet no constitutional prohibition as far as that stuff goes. At the moment I am engaged in blackmailing a pair of dirty murdering shits herewith named Andrew Neville and Claudia Dempsey, who coldly, cruelly, and greedily collaborated in slaying one John Dempsey for profit and sex. How am I doing?"

"Great."

"Are you really recording this?"

"Yes. Is your middle name really Goethe?"

"I have thus far collected considerable evidence implicating the aforementioned Andrew and Claudia in the vicious, insensate butchery of the heretofore-identified decedent John T. Dempsey. May his soul rest in peace."

"That's really good, Roland."

"Hey, I hire a temporary legal secretary to translate this shit into legal jargon. Want me to continue?"

"Please do."

"And so there you have it, members of the grand jury, of the petit jury, Your Honor, opposing counsel, citizens of this glorious and stainless republic—I freely confess to extorting substantial sums of money and sexual favors from the aforementioned Andrew and Claudia. Wait—sexual favors from the latter only, not the former. I am avaricious. Ergo sum. I am dirty. I admit it. But they are evil. And cheap. I am merely the fly in your soup. They are the scorpions in your Nikes. I appeal to you, my fellow morons, I beg you, do not allow this brutal crime, et cetera, go unavenged. The chickens must come home to roost. The angels weep! Who speaks for the victim? I speak for the victim, and now you, too, must speak for the victim; we must all speak for the poor victim who can no longer speak for himself. E pluribus unum. I am bad, but they are badder. Vox populi. Simpletons, with your just verdict you may once again thwart the barbarians at the gate and restore to America the honor and faith that the defendants would deny you. Speak resoundingly to all those who would crap all over our beloved flag. Guilty! A vote for life imprisonment is a vote for good government. We'll be serving coffee and donuts in the anteroom after your guilty verdict is rendered."

"That's powerful stuff, Roland."

"Did you really like it?"

"What can I tell you?"

"What did you think about the scorpions-in-your-Nikes line?"

"It was splendid."

"You sound bored."

"I'm not bored; I'm reverential."

"Did you tape all of it?"

"Yes."

"Will you send me a copy?"

"Sure."

"Did you like that bullshit about speaking for the victim who can no longer speak for himself?"

"You bet. Trite but true."

"I was inspired."

"It was lovely."

"But hey, I really meant that stuff about our beloved flag. Don't kid yourself, Andrew; I meant that."

"I know you did. There was a catch in your voice. The hair on the back of my head stood up."

"Listen, kid, why don't we quit this cute fucking around? Just pay me what you owe me."

"I don't owe you a dime."

"You do! Jesus, I got you cold, you and that Italian lollipop. Be a good sport; pay up, for Christ's sake. Pay your debts. It's dishonorable to snake out of a legitimate debt. I *got* you, pal."

"You don't."

"You're in denial."

"Right."

"Don't laugh. Look—how does one say it in English? Stop fucking around. This is very simple. If you were accused of a crime you'd hire a lawyer to defend you and keep you out of jail, wouldn't you? Sure you would. Well, you're a killer and I'm a lawyer. You're going to pay me to keep you and your sweet Italian antipasto out of jail. It's easy as that. Okay? Concentrate, Andrew. Hire me. I am your legal counsel; you are my client. Pay my fee. You give; I take. That's how it works. You two killers walk free, and I buy a Mercedes and a nice condo—maybe even the condo you got for sale. This is how it *works,* jerk. This is the American system of justice. Pay up, you murderous scoundrel!"

"This is becoming tedious, Roland."

"Lawyers talk and killers walk. Hey, pal? This is fun. I enjoy clowning with you, what the hell, two guys who like and understand each other, the witticisms flying—watch out; there's a zinger! Fine. It's more fun than bowling. But look, Andrew, you got to realize, I really am going to put you and the bitch away for a long time if you don't cooperate. How much—for example—how much is frequent access to that pussy worth? Huh? Separate prisons. Think about that. Yo! Andrew gang-raped in the showers. Yo! Claudia carrying on with a lesbian corrections officer. It doesn't have to be that way. Prime loin—bye-bye. The money, the *big* money and more coming in all the time—say bye-bye. Bye-bye; excuse me, I got to go make license plates. Oh, Andrew, wake up before it's too late. Share. Don't be such a greedy turd; pay your lawyer what you owe him and go off to live happily ever after."

"You live dangerously, Scheiss."

"Don't even think of it. Don't even think of taking me out."

"What do you mean? Hurt you? I would never consider such a thing."

"That remark's for the tape, right? Okay. But you see? We're making progress. You are finally beginning to take my little business proposition seriously. Good, very good. Now go and audit the books. Set aside a big number for your attorney's fee. Go then, son. Don't call me; I'll call you."

"I'll be waiting."

"Don't forget my one night of delirious carnal passion with the Italian spumoni. And, Andrew—you will send me a copy of the tape, won't you?"

SEVENTEEN

I watched professional football on the television most of the day, then at six showered and shaved and dressed for dinner. This was the first time I'd worn a suit since quitting my job. I noticed that I had lost weight, mostly around the buttocks and middle, but my face looked leaner, too. When I turned off the room lights I saw that Roland Scheiss was standing outside on the deck. You could not mistake that thick body, that neckless cannonball head. He exhaled clouds of vapor as he stared out at the lake, and he seemed to be talking to himself. I could hear the rumble of his voice, but the words made no sense.

I put on my overcoat, set the door locks, and stepped outside.

"Call your million," Scheiss was muttering. "Raise." He abruptly turned at the sound of the door closing. "Oh, hello, Andrew. I been waiting. Christ, it's cold."

"What are you doing here?"

In a fake tone of injury, he said, "I'm a Thanksgiving guest. Just like you. I was invited."

"Bullshit."

"Hey, come on; don't be that way. I thought we were pals."

"Dempsey's parents dragged you along with them."

"Boy, are you a hostile guy."

"You want to walk down the steps or do you want me to throw you over the railing?"

"I don't think you could do that, Andrew. Throw me over the railing. But"—he raised a palm—"but this is Thanksgiving, a season of harmony, of piety, of love even." He walked down the steps and stood at the bottom, staring up at me.

"Scheiss, I don't know how you've lived this long."

"It's really simple. I had a badge. I had a gun. I had a smart, and I had a mean. I still got the badge, but it don't count for much anymore. The other stuff does. Hey, pal, you gonna make me late for the turkey?"

He casually retreated as I descended the stairs. He warily matched my pace up the lawn toward the brightly lighted house. The ground was dusted with frost and frozen concrete-hard.

Scheiss, working hard to keep up, said, "Hey, Andrew, this might not bore you. I found something. I went up to Eagle's Nest and hired a bunch of Indians to search the country around where Dempsey got chopped. Three dollars an hour per head—they got no union. Guess what? Slow down. They found something. Slow down, Andrew. Not three hundred yards from the scene of the heinous crime they found what? . . . They found a deer carcass with an arrow in its gut."

"Excellent sleuthing, Roland."

"The arrow. I showed it to Harkey. You remember Harkey, don't you, or have you forgot all your old friends now that you are an intimate of the rich? Someone messed up Harkey's cabin. You remember. During the weekend that Dempsey was chopped. Mr. Harkey looks at the arrow and says, 'Yeah, yeah, that arrow comes from my cabin.' "

"So what?"

"It's a part of the picture, a piece of the mosaic. It's circumstantial. But put it together with a lot of other stuff . . ."

"What other stuff?"

"You only get to look at my *up* cards. My *down* cards stay down."

I paused at the front door and turned to face him.

He stamped his feet. "My toes are numb. I can't feel my fucking feet."

"Wipe your nose," I said. "Your nose is dripping."

"Thanks." He wiped his nose with the back of a mittened fist. "It's the cold. I got runny sinuses."

"You're a pretty dismal lesson in anatomy. Look; your investigation must have told you that I don't have much money."

"Right, you got zip now, at this moment, but soon . . ."

"Do you expect me to win the lottery?"

"Don't be coy. You *are* going to win a big lottery, my friend. You're holding a number that's coming up. Oh, Andrew, come on. Shit, man. What is this pussy act? Don't be—what's the word?—dis-in-gen-uous." He grinned.

I said, "You're smarter than you appear, but lots dumber than you think you are."

"Good. I like that. But you're underestimating me. Lots of men who underestimated me are locked in cages now or they got crushed testicles or they stutter a lot. I know tough, Andrew. You are not tough. You look at me and you laugh inside. Short, ugly, roly-poly guy with a scalp disorder, greedy, breathes hard walking up a little hill. Cheap, hustling shyster, likes his booze, weak, no way he could squeeze a man's balls until they pop, no way he could make the meanest nigger anyone ever saw stutter for the rest of his life. All right, Neville. Laugh at me. I don't care. I'm not insecure. I've got your balls in my fists, and I'm gonna squeeze, and squeeze a little more, and keep squeezing, increasing the pressure, until your faggy laugh turns into a scream."

He was either shivering from the cold or trembling with anger.

I said, "I used to think that you were like one of those harmless snakes that have markings identical to the markings of poisonous snakes. You understand? I was wrong. You really are the poisonous kind."

He was pleased. The man was pleased to hear me compare him to a poisonous snake. I could see the pleasure in his eyes and posture and shark's grin.

"But listen; a man can't have a poisonous snake hanging around the yard. You see? One simply cannot have a venomous snake around where one sleeps, eats, walks, plays, craps—you might crawl up out of the toilet bowl. Go away. Stay away."

"You finally done it; you scared me. Twenty years with the Chicago PD and I was never scared, not once. Now I am. I can feel the hot shit running down my leg. You stupid jerk. I killed two men. I would of killed six except it's so hard to kill niggers and Mexicans. They got a perverse will to live. They take their holidays in the trauma center. It's better than home; they get free drugs and free chow and clean bedsheets. You got me real scared."

"I don't want to see you around here again. Not ever."

"You gonna kill me? Hey, I ain't so easy to kill as that Dempsey. I won't show you my back. Can you kill face-to-face, Andrew?"

There were ten of us for dinner. Claudia introduced me to those guests I hadn't met: Alberto Messina, the Italian consul in Chicago, and his wife, Anna, and a middle-aged couple, the Chapmans, friends of Dempsey who owned a house on the other side of the lake and were "associated with the television industry."

Claudia had hired a woman to help with the cooking and serving and another to tend bar. I got a scotch and joined Laddy in front of the fireplace. He was wearing a tailored tux with a ruffled silk shirt, a string tie, and patent-leather shoes with three-inch heels.

"You're resplendent," I said.

"You're redundant," Laddy replied.

"You're refulgent."

"You're de trop." He pronounced the French words to rhyme with "key drop"; then he grasped my arm and sang, "Baby, if I'm the bottom, you're de trop."

He nodded toward the Dempseys and Scheiss and said, "Speaking of de trop . . . who is that pugnacious man?"

"Roland Scheiss. Don't you remember him? He was here after the funeral."

"Oh, yes. The cop-lawyer. Well, he seems to think that I'm the butler."

He knows very well who you are. The butler stuff is just his idea of wit."

"He's a homophobe, too," Laddy said. "He told me he'd never met a queer butler. He separated the syllables—butt-ler."

"Roland's a sweetheart."

"And so how are you doing, Andrew? Are you working?"

One always lied in response to that question. "Yes. I'm finishing a play."

"Are you really? Well, at last. Is it any good?"

"Yes."

"Will you let me see it when it's completed?"

"Sure."

"When will that be?"

"Sometime in the spring."

"Well, this is exciting. At last, after a silence of many years, a new play from the pen of the gifted, et cetera, brilliant, et cetera, and all that, Andrew Neville. I'm very pleased. You will let me see it, won't you? I know everybody who's anybody in the Chicago theater. I can probably even arrange a grant from my foundation. You said it's a good play?"

"Very good."

"Lovely," Laddy said. "Let me be the one who rediscovers you, Andrew."

The consul, a stocky, robust man in his middle thirties, claimed to have seen an Italian translation of my first play years ago. He praised it extravagantly. There had been a small and not very successful production in Milan in the mideighties. Messina might have seen it performed, but I was skeptical; diplomats are usually briefed on the people they expect to meet, and his interest was probably nothing more than polite flattery.

His blond wife was petite and pretty and about ten years younger than the consul. She did not speak English very well and spent most of the evening hovering near Claudia and her husband.

The Chapmans were older, fifty-something, with cloyingly sincere manners and mild opinions on every topic. Together they had created and now produced a popular daytime soap opera that Cal Chapman compared to Shakespeare: "Shakespeare for today. You know, if Shakespeare were alive now he'd be writing for television." Their house on the lake was for sale; they intended to move permanently to the Los Angeles area, "where it's all happening."

Claudia brought Dante downstairs for twenty minutes, showing him off to the guests, who fussed too much and alarmed the boy. Finally, Mrs. Dempsey hugged him so ferociously that he began to cry.

But it might have turned out a fairly pleasant evening if not for Scheiss and the Dempseys. Scheiss was Scheiss, an offensive troll in a stained three-piece suit the color and near-texture of dirty straw. He was careful to omit no one from his sly insults.

The Dempseys were cold, remote, disapproving. They did not mingle with the other guests. They spoke to each other and to Scheiss in whispers. They glared. They, like Roland Scheiss, exercised the only power they possessed: the power to make people uncomfortable or unhappy or angry.

Claudia had worked hard. There was a variety of food and wine, all of it good; Laddy was at first chipper and witty, the consul charming, the Chapmans interested if not interesting; but it was no use—the mood had been fouled.

During dinner I noticed that Scheiss was displaying a new gold Rolex watch and, on the left little finger of the same hand, a ring with a square-cut ruby that had to weigh at least two carats. Roland was prospering or expected to prosper soon.

Halfway through the meal he stood up and, smirking, said, "Excuse me; I forgot to wash my hands."

When he did not soon return I got up and went out into the big room. Scheiss was slowly descending the staircase.

"Ah, Andrew, my friend," he said. "Did you neglect to wash up, too?"

The bedrooms were upstairs: Claudia's suite, Dante's room, and, adjoining that, the quarters of the live-in girl.

"Those Arabs got the right idea. They wipe with their left hands and eat with their right. But I can never remember which hand is which, so I got to wash both of them." He grinned, came down the stairs, brushed past me, and returned to the dining room.

The girl told me that Scheiss had opened her door, apologized, and said that he was looking for a bathroom.

"Did he enter Dante's room?" I asked.

"No."

"Did he go into Claudia's rooms?"

Yes, he had entered Claudia's suite (the girl could hear him thumping around in there) and remained for maybe five minutes. It bothered her, but she did not think that she had the authority to protest this invasion by one of Claudia's guests.

"It's all right," I said.

"He scared me. I didn't like the way he looked at me."

"No one does, Mary. Don't worry; he won't come up here again."

The two hired women had been dismissed early, and so I stayed to help clean the place. Then Claudia brewed a pot of coffee and we sat together on a sofa facing the fireplace. I found her more beautiful now than at the beginning of the evening, with her smoky hair tousled and her makeup a bit smeared and her eyelids slightly puffy. When perfectly groomed, Claudia had that slick magazine cover beauty that denies individuality. Now she removed her shoes and earrings. She leaned her head back against the cushion and half-closed her eyes.

"Was it awful?" she asked.

"Awkward at times, but not awful."

"It's so hard to do the simplest things in this country. There is always conflict, always discontent."

"Really, it wasn't so bad, Claudia," I lied. "The Messinas and the Chapmans and Laddy enjoyed themselves."

"That diabolical little man . . ."

"Scheiss, yes—nasty."

"He wasn't invited, you know."

"I assumed that."

"The Dempseys brought him without asking me. Oh, I'll never have anything more to do with them. I don't care if they are John's parents and Dante's grandparents. Disagreeable, perverse little plebeians."

"Spoilers," I said.

"Do you know what he said to me, this Scheiss? He said—I still can't believe it—he said that soon he would be filing papers with the court to take Dante away from me. He said I was not a fit mother. He said those things to me, smiling his dirty smile."

"He went upstairs during dinner."

"Upstairs?"

"I followed him. Mary said that he had gone into your rooms."

"Dante!" she cried, and she swiftly rose and ran up the stairs.

I took my coffee cup to the bar and poured in an ounce of brandy. It was very windy outside; the coals in the fireplace dimmed and brightened in response to the chimney drafts. You could feel a chill when you moved away from the fire.

Claudia came down the stairs.

"Dante is all right, isn't he?"

"That vile, disgusting man. He left—he used the toilet. He left a . . . a *stool* in the toilet."

"He would. Of course he would."

"Oh, I don't like it here. I want to go home."

"Where is home?"

"Tuscany, Siena, but I think I'll live in Florence when I go back."

"Florence is beautiful."

"You have been there? Oh, yes, it is beautiful. I am not happy in this country, Andrew. When John was alive . . . But now, no, I don't understand Americans at all."

"Have you seen a real estate agent about selling the property?"

"No. I find it so difficult to act. To take action. You understand? I feel burdened, burdened by this house and the farm and the house in Malibu, by all the property and possessions, by sadness, by anger, by . . . by futility."

"I'll help you, if you wish. I can interview some real estate people for you."

"Would you? Yes. Please, yes, help me lose these burdens so that Dante and I can go home."

"I'll start tomorrow."

"Yes, help me. I feel better already."

"Good. Leave it to me, then."

"Yes. I shall. I really do feel better. My mind has been so cluttered. Would you like some more coffee? A drink?"

"It's late. I should go."

"Tomorrow one of those charities—Goodwill?—is coming to take away John's clothes and things. They're very good clothes, very expensive. You are about his size. Would you like to look through everything before they take it away?"

"All right."

She walked me to the front door and impulsively embraced

me and kissed my cheek. It was a brief, light embrace, a gentle, warm pressure. I could feel her warmth and softness and smell her hair and skin and feel the pressure of her lips on my cheek.

"Good night," she said. "Thank you. You are a good friend, Andrew."

EIGHTEEN

That night I had the first of the headaches. It wasn't extremely painful, just a burning at the temples and base of the skull, but even so it worried me—it was the first headache of my life. I had been doing a lot of close work; perhaps the headache resulted from eyestrain. I made an appointment with an opthalmologist.

Dempsey had owned a great amount of clothing, and everything was first-rate in quality and cut. I didn't want Claudia to think me greedy, and so I took only a third of what I wanted: a couple of Harris tweed sport coats, a blue suit tailored in London, shirts made in Jermyn Street, cashmere sweaters, two pairs of shoes lasted in Italy, and a Burberry raincoat. Everything fit fairly well, and would fit perfectly when I lost a few more pounds.

An opthalmologist examined my eyes and concluded that I was slightly myopic. Was this myopia the source of my headache? Probably not. After all, a single headache . . . I selected frames like the ones Dempsey had worn, gold aviator type with a very faint amber tint to the lenses. The headaches did not cease.

My mustache had grown out. I stalked back and forth in front of the mirror, wearing Dempsey's clothes and eyeglasses exactly like those he had worn and with a mustache shaped like his, and I could feel John Dempsey entering me, leaving his grave and entering me.

My hair was coming in gray at the temples. I took a photograph of Dempsey to a hairstylist and had my hair darkened and cut like his, thick and feathery hair that hardly required combing.

There were moments when I could hear Dempsey's speech rhythms and the timbre of his voice in my own voice, and I knew that in part I was being occupied by him. Not possessed. I was still Andrew Neville, mostly Neville, but Dempsey too. He lived through me; I lived through him. I had seized his life.

Claudia knew. It was never mentioned, but she could hardly fail to notice how much I now resembled her beloved John. The clothes, the eyeglasses, hairstyle, mustache, the voice and gestures and careless charm—she knew, all right, and I believe that she was secretly glad to have her husband returned to her even in this counterfeit form. Her grief and loss were so great that she collaborated in the deception.

Astarte knew. I believed that the falcon knew. And little Dante—the boy became less suspicious of me; he began to trust. There were moments when he was shyly affectionate. Once he called me "Da." Claudia did not correct him. She had been infected; we were engaged in a folie à deux.

Each morning I spent twenty or thirty minutes trying to access Dempsey's script on the computer. I moved deeper and deeper toward cryptography, trying ever more arcane combinations of words and numbers. It seemed a futile quest; why, after all, would he elect to conceal a film script while leaving available a personal journal?

In early December I carried a mug of coffee to the desk, switched on the computer, and in sequence typed: "SCRIPT; FILM SCRIPT; MOVIE SCRIPT; TV SCRIPT." Nothing. Probably there was no script of any kind; maybe he had not proceeded beyond the note-taking stage. "NOVEL." No. "STORY; SHORT STORY; NOVELLA." No. "PLAY."

Last Night at Marie's
(A Play in Three Acts)
by
John Dempsey

There were five characters of consequence in the play: two couples, the Wrights and the Olivers, who are gathered at the Wrights' house for a small dinner party, and one Charles Neville. Neville, a new acquaintance, was expected to bring his wife, but he arrives alone and offers vague and inconsistent explanations for her absence. She can be expected soon. She is en route. But she does not appear, and during the course of the evening Neville refers to her as Susan, Suzanne, and Lucille and seems to be talking about a different woman each time. One begins to wonder if Neville murdered his wife earlier in the evening (as the others suspect), or if Susan-Suzanne-Lucille does not really exist and is just another lie in the elaborate fantasy that Neville constructs during the course of the night. He is a gentle inquisitor, an unreliable raconteur, a tempter, and there is a vague sense of menace in his every gesture and utterance.

The Wrights and Olivers are at first portrayed as extremely dull, conventional, humorless, self-important fools. They speak in clichés and platitudes. They serve as a sort of chorus to each other, murmuring, "Yes," or, "Exactly," or, "Indeed," to each banality. The are comically banal. They are insincerely sincere. But layer after layer of their individual and collective hypocrisy is worn away by Neville's subtle provocations; they behave more and more erratically, and there are abrupt explosions of fury, weeping, wild accusations, and finally violence as at last they unite to murder Neville.

At that point the doorbell rings. Neville's wife—Lucinda—enters and apologizes for arriving so late. The others, now again dull, conventional, humorless, reassure her, offer her food and l sit and politely chat over the unmentioned s the curtain descends.

comic play. Not very original: the play was npsey, one-fifth Harold Pinter, and three- w Neville. I was surprised to see how deeply influenced Dempsey had been by my own two produced plays, *Let Them Dance* and *Payback*. He had obviously used them as models. *Last Night at Marie's* was not legally a plagiarism, though it could hardly be considered original; my "signature" (and, to a lesser extent, Harold Pinter's) was present throughout. It contained my rhythms, my themes, my wit, my sort of situation, and the characters were the kind that I myself might have chosen. But oddly, at the same time, his play was potentially much better than either of mine because Dempsey possessed what I'd always lacked: an unerring sense of form. He had constructed his play as methodically as an architect would design a high-rise; the framework was strong, balanced, and invisible.

The third act was too long by about five minutes and too frantic while leading toward the quiet denouement—Dempsey had lost confidence, lost control, and so wrote most of the last act as conventional farce. True, there were farcical aspects, but they had to be played fairly straight. And there were lines to be cut, other lines sharpened, new lines to be written.

It was a good play as written; it would be very good when I completed my revisions. So then, Dempsey and I were collaborators, though his name would not appear on the script or marquee.

The use of my surname for Dempsey's central character was curious. A coincidence, perhaps—Neville was not an unusual name; you'd find at least a few in even a small telephone directory. And of course John and I had been closely acquainted, near friends, twenty years ago. Yet he could hardly have based his strange Mephistophelian Charles on the rather simple and decent boy I was then. There was not necessarily an association bet Charles Neville and Andrew Neville. Still, the use of my surna might have been a sly acknowledgment of my influence on his play, a bow toward me, a sort of homage. *Homage* was a word used in Hollywood to justify plagiarism.

None of that mattered. What mattered was that after a long drought, years of creative sterility, I was working on a new play, a fine play. I was reborn.

NINETEEN

"Hey, buddy, how're you doing?"

"Pretty good."

"Miss your old pal?"

"You bet."

"You wasn't worried you wouldn't hear from me again?"

"*Worried* isn't the word. I've been desolate. I just sit here and cry, waiting for the phone to ring."

"Well, it rung finally."

"And I'm so grateful."

"I've been traveling. Milwaukee, Green Bay, Eagle's Nest."

"Ah, the Grand Tour."

"You know what I like about you, Andrew?"

"I'm afraid to ask."

"You got balls."

"Oh, that."

"No, I mean you do. Got balls."

"Your manly approval means so much to me."

"I mean, people think a killer automatically got guts. It takes guts to kill. Nah. Mostly it's sneaky. It ain't guts; usually, it's booze or dope or the dumb wino bum turned his back. It's I got a gun and he only got a soft body. I got a knife; he ain't looking. You know? Usually it's about I drop a brick on the head of the snotty kid down on the sidewalk. It's I get mad when the crippled old lady don't turn over her Social Security bucks fast enough. It's here comes the train; why don't I push this chick onto the tracks to see what it's like? Impulse murder—you see a lot of that these days. Look at that fucking yuppie bicycler. I hate him, think I'll twist the wheel of my five-thousand-pound Vindictiva. You know? There's a lot of resentment out there. It's put rat poison in the senile old fart's soup. It's I got to hurt this bitch bad in order to make her into a better human being. It's, hey, killing something weak is the only way I can get off. It's if that baby don't stop crying soon . . ."

"Are we coming to the point?"

"Alls I'm saying, alluding to, is that you at least had the balls to kill a healthy man face-to-face. Well, no, not exactly, more like partly face-to-back and partly face-to-face. That's according to the coroner. Dempsey had a knife, too. He was butchering a deer, and he had a big knife. He was armed, right? It was almost like a duel. Not much, I guess, but a little like that. He wasn't ready, he didn't expect your sudden frenzy, but even so, he wasn't a quadriplegic and he had a knife. What I'm saying, Andrew, is that you're a cut above—*mon dieu,* forgive the pun!—a cut above the common ordinary cowardly garden variety killer. You got status with me, pal."

"Yes. And . . . ?"

"And. Well, Dempsey cut you during the slaughter, just a little nick, probably, but they found human human blood with the deer blood on Dempsey's knife. You wiped the blade, but that ain't enough for the modern labs; they found it. Your blood, old buddy boy. You ever hear of DNA testing?"

"Yes, and I've heard bullshit before, too."

"He nicked you with his knife during the monumental struggle."

"Did he?"

"Well, a little of your saliva or blood, a strand of your hair, and your DNA can be matched up with the blood on John's knife. What do you think of them apples?"

"Horseapples. It's all bluff, Scheiss, but nice try. Are you finished now?"

"Almost. But I got to ask—how is the tender wop getting along?"

"Do you want to talk dirty for a while?"

"Sure, but I'd rather *do* dirty."

"Of course."

"What I wonder, what does she think of me, Andrew? Tell the truth. Does she find me disgusting?"

"Loathsome."

"Really? That kind of revulsion often contains a high erotic content. You're laughing. I made you laugh. *Loathsome*—is that her word?"

"Yes. Loathsome. Hideous. Maggoty. That sort of thing."

"Well, there it is. She's got the hots for me."

"I'm going to hang up now, Roland. But don't think I'm not appreciative of your keeping in touch."

"Wait. Does she ever idly speculate on the dimensions of my male member?"

"Good-bye, Roland."

"Wait. You don't buy your blood on Dempsey's knife?"

"No."

"It don't matter. I got lots of other stuff besides that."

"Good for you. Keep in touch, now."

TWENTY

Each morning when I awakened, the lake was invisible beneath white clouds of vapor that rose a hundred yards into the air before dissolving. It looked like the smoke from a vast prairie fire. The comparatively warm lake water reacted to the very cold air by exhaling those seething crystalline clouds. The pond and the little creek smoked, too.

One morning I saw that a thin shell of ice extended thirty yards out from shore. The ice was about a quarter of an inch thick and as clear as window glass. The lake still smoked farther out. I saw flights of geese descend into the mist and vanish. The gulls had gone, but geese and ducks and coots arrived from the north every day. When the sun dispersed the vapor I could see them floating far out on the dark blue lake.

Each day the ice was a little thicker and extended farther into open water. When it was about two inches thick I ventured out. It had a sort of rubbery flex, sagging a little and creaking beneath my weight. I stayed away from the mouth of the brook; moving water would thin the ice, weaken it. The ice had frozen smooth and clear, and I could see the bottom without distortion. I passed over rock-filled cribs, buoy anchors, weed beds and sandy patches, snail and clam shells, shards of colored glass, an old fishing lure, and what looked like a tackle box half buried in the silt. And there were fish, most of them small.

SPLIT IMAGE

By Christmas week the ice was four inches thick, and ramshackle fishing hut villages appeared off the three lakeside towns. A large oval of open water remained in the center of the lake, and there were still flocks of geese that flew off to forage in the cornfields during the day and return at dusk. Iceboats appeared: they moved swiftly even in a light wind, masts raked back, sails taut, the runners scraping long curved scars on the dark ice.

Daylight was brief, about nine hours from sunrise to sunset, and the weak sun—you could stare directly at it—arced low above the southern horizon. The sky, too, was pale, more green than blue, and the clouds gray. It was always cold, often windy, dark until eight in the morning and dark again a little after four. The lake froze completely except for a network of seams that zigzagged from shore to shore across the middle of the lake. Sometimes one seam froze over and another opened.

At night I lay in bed and listened to the groans, moans, pings, rumbles, and cracks of the expanding ice. The sounds were amplified, reverberant. The lake was rarely silent. At times I was suddenly awakened by great detonations as pressure fractured the ice, resonant cracks as loud as thunder. I could feel the vibrations on my skin. Dishes rattled in a cupboard.

I didn't sleep well. There were the noises, like the rending of the planet, and headaches, and there were my dreams, as vivid as hallucinations. Dempsey never actually appeared in the early dreams, although he dominated them. He was always present. Now and then, half-asleep and dimly aware of the fierce growling of the lake, I would believe, be certain, that they were not my dreams but his. The dreams of a corpse now decomposing in his expensive dark suit, in his fine shiny ebony and silk and bronze coffin.

In the early morning, dulled by lack of sleep and the emotional dreams, I would sit by the frosted window and sip coffee and think: The deeper mind does not know about death, does not recognize it; no one dies in its timeless realm until you die—then all die. Dempsey will not return. He cannot possess you. Remember? You are engaged in possessing him.

Later in the morning I would walk the grounds, my domain now, and see Claudia and Dante, and my fatigue would evaporate into a flash of happiness. Sometimes I feared that my daytime happiness was more dangerous than my nighttime depression. The happiness was equally capable of consuming me.

The cemetery was buried beneath eight or ten inches of snow. Crusty drifts had formed against the headstones and fences. The bare black tree limbs meshed overhead and ice-coated twigs tinkled like tiny bells in the wind. Small round birds, their feathers puffed, flitted about in avian panic when we entered.

The flagstone walks hadn't been shoveled. No one had visited recently; there were no footprints or flowers or wreaths. With each step my boot broke through the hard crust and into the powder snow beneath. Claudia, carrying Dante piggyback, followed.

We found the grave and stood at its foot, looking down, looking for Dempsey in a way, but there was nothing but the snow and frozen earth and the pretentious gravestone. A cemetery seems an even lonelier place in winter, as desolate as the extinction it conceals. Here the corpses lay side by side and head to foot. I recalled a story by Gogol in which the dead talked among themselves at night. They told stories, mournful, comic, and banal stories.

Claudia pointed at the adjoining grave plot. "That's mine. I bought it."

"Did you? Why?"

"I don't know. I was so unhappy, so muddled, and the salesman was very persuasive. I won't be buried here. I hate this place."

Back in the car she said, "I won't return. John isn't here."

No. But he was at least partially within me, in a way I could not explain or hardly even imagine.

Now late at night, while half-awake and half-asleep, tortured by a headache, drugged on painkillers, I sensed Dempsey's arrival. He came to me stinking of the grave. While the expanding ice howled and thundered, Dempsey came, and I could feel his icy breath on my cheek. "Why? *Why?*" he would whisper. "Andrew, how could you steal my precious life, all my days, Claudia, my son . . ."

He was not always accusing. Often he would whisper advice. "Andrew, you are too gentle with Claudia, too worshipful, and too cold—she is passionate and requires passion in return. Passion, Andrew!"

And: "You can't buy Dante's affection with toy trains and model airplanes, nor with deferential words. Be firm but true."

One night he even admonished me about my changes in his play. "You are mutilating my drama, Andrew. For Christ's sake, leave it as it is!

"Oh, it's so cold in the grave, so cold in the dark, in my fancy box with its absurd little pillow, in my seven-foot-deep by three-foot-wide rectangle of frozen earth, in my confinement, in my isolation and decay. . . . Let me warm myself at your fire for a moment; then I'll go. I promise I'll go. . . ."

But he didn't go, not all of him; some part of John Dempsey infiltrated me with each hallucinatory visitation.

"Andrew, take Claudia to Italy. She doesn't belong here. Take her and Dante to Florence; take us all to Florence."

During the daylight hours I understood that Dempsey's 3:00 A.M. visits were dreams, hallucinations, but at night I wasn't sure. It was all so plausible. I recognized the timbre of his voice and the cadence of his speech, smelled his sewery grave-breath, felt his icy touch, agreed with or disputed his assertions. We quarreled. John was a bully.

"Listen," Dempsey said, "you know, don't you, that we've got to kill Roland Scheiss."

It remained very cold. Birds gathered around the rims of chimneys to warm themselves. At night you could hear tree limbs splitting from the cold.

One morning in early January I awakened and saw that an ice-fishing shack had been situated fifty yards offshore. It had been hauled in during the night. There were no other shacks in the area. I observed it for several days. Twice I saw smoke boiling out of the chimney pipe, but I never saw a car, did not see anyone arrive or depart.

After breakfast on Tuesday, I dressed warmly and walked out on the ice. The fishing shack was small, about eight feet by ten, built with a frame of two-by-fours covered with plywood and then painted a dull primer red. There were windows on all four sides, but the curtains—fashioned out of old army blankets—were tightly drawn. A sooty stovepipe stuck up through the roof. The hut was on wooden runners so that it could easily be dragged across the ice. The door was secured by a combination lock.

I walked back to the boathouse for a screwdriver, returned, and removed the screws from the steel hasp.

It was dim inside the hut and smelled of kerosene and stale cigar smoke. Several cigars had been crushed out in a coffee can. There was an old iron heating stove, a gallon of fuel, another gallon can of white gasoline, a gas pressure lantern, a wooden chair seat cushion that spilled foam, and an overturned wooden crate. Under the crate I found a small coffeepot, coffee, a bag of chocolate Kisses, a pint of sour mash whiskey, and half a dozen pornographic magazines. Scheiss's tastes were eclectic: two of the magazines featured male orgiasts.

When I lifted the trapdoor a greenish light filtered up through the square of exposed ice and trembled on the walls. I could hear distant submarine groans and rumbles.

Through the dirty south window you could see the house, the boathouse, and much of the property. A good telephoto or zoom lense would draw everything close, right into the hut, in fact, and into your camera. And you could record conversations picked up by the bugs you'd planted in Claudia's room on the night of the Thanksgiving dinner. You could sit in the warmth and drink whiskey-laced coffee and smoke cheap cigars and lazily page through the crotch magazines until something onshore aroused your professional interest.

TWENTY-ONE

Scheiss did not use the fishing shack during the week, but on Saturday night he was there. It was a little after nine o'clock when I saw smoke, thickened by the cold, boiling out of the stovepipe. A thin vertical line of light bisected the window curtain. He was out there. I hadn't seen him arrive, but he was there now. That he would come out on a night like this was evidence of his determination, his furious, mad-dog, stupid will. It was very cold, ten below zero, with a bitter wind blowing out of the northwest. There was no moon, no clouds. It would have been totally dark if not for the snow that reflected starlight with a dim, misty radiance. Cold, windy, dark, even dangerous—a man could quickly freeze to death on such a night.

I dressed slowly in the dark: a sweat suit, jeans, a wool shirt, a wool sweater, a knit ski cap, my down jacket with its hood, two pairs of wool socks, hiking boots, and mittens, both leather and wool. I slipped an iron crowbar down my right hip between the sweat suit pants and the jeans. It was smooth and heavy, with a clefted hook at one end and a curved pry-blade at the other. Even wearing all those clothes, I could immediately feel the damp, vicious cold when I went outside.

I walked far out into the bleak arctic wastes, almost to the lake's center, and then circled back toward shore. The fishing shack was a distant blocky shadow that leaked trickles of light. And ahead and well to my left, just a sprinkle of gleams on chrome and glass, was Roland Scheiss's car.

The expanding ice resounded with a demonic orchestra of noise—groans, growls, rumbles, pings, cracks like rifle shots, cracks like thunder, all amplified and reverberating through the water below. And I heard a sourceless wind-teased music woven into the dissonance of rending ice, so faint and intermittent that I could not be sure it existed anywhere but in my mind. But when I approached the hut I recognized the music as the soprano aria "Tu che i miseri conforti," from *Tancredi.*

I moved close to the back window and peered through a burn hole in the curtain. The pane was steamy, but I could see well enough. A gasoline pressure lantern hanging from a nail filled the shack with a hard white glare. Scheiss was sitting hunched at the card table, his back to me. He wore a bulky insulated blue jump-suit, a navy watch cap, and a long yellow muffler. On the table lay a liter bottle of whiskey, a stack of paper cups, an ashtray that contained a smoldering cigar, his revolver, and a shiny, elaborate piece of electronic equipment about the size of a cracker box. Its face was covered with dials and lights and switches. The opera that Claudia was listening to in her room issued from the box.

I walked around to the front of the shack and knocked on the door.

Music ceased, and after a prolonged silence Scheiss said, "Who?"

"Neville."

"Who?"

"Your pal. Neville."

Another brief silence and then, "On a night not fit for man nor beast, comes Andrew. What do you want?"

"I want to talk to you."

"Lift the latch bar and push," he said. "And let your empty hands enter first."

I went into the shack and closed the door behind me. Scheiss was standing against the far wall. The revolver was in his hand, but he wasn't pointing it at me.

"Well," he said. "How do you like my little winter vacation chalet?"

"I'm impressed."

"I bought it from an old man for ninety-five bucks."

"A steal," I said.

He smiled, observing me with his wary pig eyes, and then said, "Drat! Where are my manners? Sit down, my friend. Draw that crate up close to my welcoming hearth. May I serve you a beverage?"

"Yes." I sat on the crate next to the kerosene heater.

Scheiss set his gun on the table, poured whiskey into a paper cup, and gave it to me.

"Ah," he said. "A cheery blaze, a warming cup of grog, hearty masculine companionship. What could be finer on a cruel winter night?"

"Nothing, Roland."

"Indeed, nothing." He sat down at the card table, half-turned to watch me, his hand a few inches from the revolver.

It was very hot in the little room. Patches of the iron stove had overheated and glowed a cherry red. The fire burned orange and blue behind the quartz window. The trapdoor in the floor was open. Scheiss had been fishing as well as spying; a short spinning rod lay on the floorboards, its line slanting down into the luminous jade-green water. A ten-inch perch lay in the corner, its eye staring blankly upward, a gill slowly opening and closing. It gleamed a flecked yellow-gold in the lantern light. The small dying fish dominated the cluttered space, drew the eye.

"Well," Scheiss said, "you have a libation—will you also share my humble fare?"

"No thanks."

"I have—let me inventory—I have chocolate Kisses, corn chips, fried pork rinds, and . . . yes, a cheese Danish."

"I'm not hungry."

"Alas."

I wondered how long he would persist in this heavy and humorless irony. The whiskey was a cheap sour mash bourbon, raw and burning.

"Well, anyhow, we must smoke together. Have a cigar, Andrew."

"No."

"You must. It's part of the masculine ritual."

"No."

"Take it, Andrew."

"No."

"Please?"

I shook my head.

"I really do insist."

Evidently Scheiss saw this cigar business as a demonstration of will, a crude ceremony of dominance.

"No," I said. "And no again."

"You offend me. No civilized man would refuse a symbol of amity such as this cigar represents."

"No civilized man would smoke one of your cigars."

He gave up, leaned back in the chair, and tilted his scarred face toward the ceiling. "Okay," he said. "What the fuck do you want?"

"A deal."

"Show me a card."

"You first."

"Ace," Scheiss said. "The arrow my crew of Indians found in a deer not far from where Dempsey got chopped. An old wood arrow that matches exactly the arrows found in Mr. Harkey's cabin, which cabin is only a few miles from the scene of the slaughter. You and Harkey worked together, were friends. He offered you the use of his cabin. There is a definite linkage. Ace."

"You've already shown me that card."

"It's a good one."

"You can't place me anywhere near the murder."

"Your photographs have been circulated in and around Eagle's Nest, Andrew lad. Someone might recognize you. Maybe a skinny Indian kid who works in a gas station remembers a guy what bought some gas and worried about the roads. Maybe another guy says, 'Hey, yeah, this is the guy what had a few beers in my joint.' Maybe two guys from Milwaukee met the guy in the photograph in the woods, saw blood all over him. Said he'd just gutted a deer. Carrying an old bow and some old wooden arrows, he was."

"How did you find them?"

"I'm good, Andrew, very good. And I work very hard. And I hire good people to help me. You talk to people, you show them a picture of a man, you buy the guest lists from all the motels and lodges for that particular weekend, and you make phone calls, hundreds of phone calls, and you do the legwork and the scut work."

"Not bad, Roland."

"Gotcha!"

"Hardly. You've got junk."

"Maybe there's more, pal."

"What?"

"Hey, am I the only chap showing his cards?"

I nodded toward his machine. "You bugged Claudia's bedroom the night of the Thanksgiving party."

"You got me on that, pal."

"You thought you'd tape us discussing the crime, confessing, implicating ourselves."

"The thought occurred to me."

"Does that machine retrieve tapes from the house?"

"It cost me eighteen hundred dollars."

"Aren't you disappointed? You haven't recorded us making love or talking about the murder—you've recorded opera. Claudia listens to an opera nearly every night. This has done wonders for your musical education, Roland."

"Let's quit dancing. I got enough right now to get you indicted for murder one. But I don't want to put you and your wop darling in jail. I merely want to share the wealth."

"I don't think any DA would indict us on what you have."

"Then I'll get more. You killed Dempsey, Andrew, butchered him. You know it and I know it and you know I know it. So stop being coy."

"I killed him," I said.

Only a brief hesitation revealed his surprise at my admission.

"Okay, fine," he said. "Finally we're on the road to Xanadu."

"But Claudia had nothing to do with it."

"Now that's an honorable thing to say. I appreciate and admire your gallantry; I really do. I'll even pretend to believe you during our mutually profitable association. Claudia had nothing to do with the murder of her husband? She's as innocent as a newborn lamb? Fine, Andrew. I'm easy."

"I didn't know Claudia until after I'd killed Dempsey."

"I told you I'm easy. I believe you."

"I don't know how it happened that I killed him. I certainly don't know why. It was some sort of incredible accident."

"Accident? Sure. Sure it was. The knife slipped. It can happen to anyone."

"The estate is tied up in probate."

"I'm a lawyer, remember? I know all about that probate shit. But she can take out a loan easy. I need a little walking-around cash. This has been an expensive operation. I got bills; I got debts; I hired associates I got to pay. Ten thousand dollars tomorrow—as a token of your generous instinct, good-faith money.

"Tomorrow is Sunday."

"Monday then. I'm flexible."

"All right. How much do you want altogether?"

"How does one-third of everything sound?"

"It sounds far too greedy. Impossible. I'll arrange in time to give you $100,000."

"Hey! Did you think we were negotiating? We're not. One-third of all Dempsey's assets, solid, liquid, and gaseous. After all, I'm one of you now, a partner, a coconspirator even. We three are all together in the same bed, Andrew, figuratively speaking. Which reminds me—you haven't forgot my big condition? I get one night alone with Claudia. She'll probably like it. I can get her body to enjoy what her mind deplores. That's the deal."

"I'll tell her. But it's up to Claudia."

When I stood up, he recoiled, snatched his revolver, and aimed it at me. His face was flushed from the heat and whiskey and his sense of triumph.

"Take it easy," I said. "I'm going."

"Aren't you going to call me bad names?"

"You know what you are."

"And I know what you are, you and that cold-blooded—what? What is the name for her, Andrew?"

"Vixen?" I said.

He laughed. "Vixen. I like that. Vixen will do. Bold vixen. Yes."

"I'll get the 10,000 for you on Monday. Where are you staying?"

"Oh, no, pal. Uh-huh. I'll phone you."

"Very well. Good night, and thanks for the cheap booze and cheap talk."

"Hey, pal, wait. I got to commend you on your new persona. Speak of cheap—you look like Dempsey's low-life psychopathic brother."

TWENTY-TWO

The doors of Scheiss's car were locked, and so I could not wait inside, out of the wind. Grains of wind-blown snow swarmed over the ice. The moisture in my nostrils froze. My exhalations condensed and turned into frost, then ice, in my mustache. Above, constellations vanished behind dirty, swiftly moving clouds and then star-by-star reappeared.

Light still burned behind the shack's window curtains. What was keeping Scheiss? Did he intend to drink and fish (and listen to opera) late into the night? Come on, Roland. Your time has come.

The tire iron was heavy and cold. The coldness of the steel was conducted through my leather outer and wool inner mittens, numbing the tips of my fingers. If he did not come soon I would have to postpone it. "It"—murder. I couldn't remember much about the first one except as illuminated in certain highly symbolic dreams and their coded emotions.

The ice creaked and ticked and pinged. There had not been any of the thunderous cracks for some time. Now and then the wind gusted so powerfully that the car rocked on its suspension.

Finally the shack's door opened, spilling a buttery trapezoid of light over the ice. A dwarfish shadow appeared. The wind diminished, and in the lull I could hear the crunch of his steps crossing a frozen patch of snow. It was fairly quiet now except for the periodic slamming of the shack's door.

His shadowy form was close now. I could hear his labored breathing. I heard the key scratch against metal. I heard him mutter something, and then the door opened (activating the dome light), and I rushed around the back of the car with the tire iron raised.

Scheiss's moon-round face was pale in the dim light, his eyes wide. He had his right hand on the open door; his left held the recorder case. "What?" he said. "What?" His terror was a stimulus. The iron landed squarely high on the left side of his head. He dropped the case and staggered away. "No," he said. "Please don't." I hit him again and he fell to his knees, and then almost immediately rose again.

He said something that made no sense. He talked. His voice was choked and he babbled in an unknown tongue. He stood before me, his feet wide apart, swaying, his face masked by blood, and he spewed out a kind of querulous babytalk. His damaged brain manufactured nonexistent syllables, words, and phrases. Then, as if he had made his position clear, he staggered away, and I hit him again with the iron bar and he collapsed facedown on the ice. He keened, and his limbs jerked paroxysmally, and then at last he was still.

I closed the car door, switching off the interior light, and leaned against the front fender. I was exhausted. I had moved no more than ten yards and swung the tire iron three times, and yet I was exhausted.

The lake rumbled, snapped. The wind gusted. My ears resonated with Scheiss's shouts and senseless babble and the particular sound the tire iron made striking his skull. The violence seemed to continue in a distant realm or dimension. (As for me, Dempsey's death was incessantly recurring elsewhere.) Gradually the echoes became more and more remote until they were merely insinuations of the wind.

The shack's door periodically slammed with a crack like a pistol shot.

I doubted that we had been heard. The noises of wind and the rending ice were loud. Only a few of the houses were occupied in this season, and no one would be outdoors tonight. The light in Claudia's upstairs room had been extinguished.

"Roland," I said. "You knew I was a killer. You *knew* it."

I crossed the stretch of ice and entered the shack. It was still relatively warm inside. Tomorrow I must drive my car out onto the ice, "neutralize" the shack, and then drag it to another part of the lake. Roland's "vacation chalet." Roland's pigsty. In this light the perch on the floor looked as if it had been chiseled out of gold. A blind eye stared upward; the tail fin curled feebly as I watched. I turned off the stove and the gas pressure lantern, shut and locked the door, and walked back to the car.

For an instant I thought that Scheiss had escaped. Skull crushed, senselessly babbling, he had somehow risen and staggered off across the lake. But smears of blood led me around to the other side of the car. His revolver lay on the ice. His boots protruded from beneath the car. Poor Scheiss—no place to hide.

I grasped his ankles and dragged him belly-down out onto the ice. He expelled a soft, bubbly moan. Perhaps it was only air escaping the corpse's lungs. Perhaps he was still alive. I did not have the heart to hit him again with the iron bar.

In his pockets I found his wallet, a jackknife, a packet of cigars and a Zippo lighter, and a key to a motel at the east end of the lake.

Scheiss was not really fat, as I'd supposed; he was thickly, solidly fleshed, like a swine, and much heavier than his height suggested. It required considerable effort to lift him into the front passenger seat of his car.

The engine refused to start. Cold had drained the battery and thickened the oil. The starter was slow. "Maintain your goddamned vehicle, Roland," I said furiously. I switched off the ignition, waited five minutes, and tried it again. The engine caught, ran very roughly for a time, and then smoothed out. Cold air blew in through the heater vents. My breath fogged the windshield. I saw that the gas gauge's indicator needle lay just above the empty mark. Bloody Roland, slumped in the seat, moaned softly. I was still cold, but at least out of the wind now, and soon the heater would begin issuing warm air.

I drove slowly toward the northeast, toward the deepest part of the lake. Surely one of the network of seams would be open or at least not thickly frozen. There were a few stars, a few lights burning here and there in the black hills cupping the lake. Gusts of wind rocked the car. Every fifty yards or so I switched on the headlights.

"Dangerous," I said. "Got to be careful. Don't want to go into the icy drink with you, pal, much as I like you."

Now I was exhilarated; I felt absolutely free, unchained from custom and convention, unintimidated by death, my own or another's. I was beyond all of that.

The ice flexed beneath the weight of the car, cracking and singing. I flashed the lights and at their limit saw a glint of black water. The brakes locked when I hit the pedal and the car slowly described a 360-degree angle before finally halting.

I got out of the car and cautiously advanced. The seam was about thirty feet wide and mostly frozen over, though here and there patches of water wrinkled and swirled. The bottom was 140 feet below. Dark down there, and cold, a lonely voyage for Roland. But he would not remain there forever. Eventually—possibly next summer—sport divers would discover the car. They would spiral down out of light into the layers of darkness, and they would see a glint of chrome or glass and timidly gaze in through a window at the bloated corpse.

I walked back, shifted the transmission into Drive, and slammed the door. Bye-bye. The tires spun without traction for a moment, and then the car was moving forward. It was halfway across the seam, slewing sideways, when the shell of new ice fractured. It settled into the water with a ponderous grace, shards of ice tinkling like wind chimes, floated there for an instant canted to the left, then nose-first began to sink.

And then there was a freakish short circuit in the car's electrical system; all of the lights came on, the horn blew, the radio loudly blared, the four side windows rolled down, and a gray shape—the safety air bag—ballooned.

Lights continued to glow as the car submerged. I watched them descend five feet, ten, the headlights piercing deep into blackness and taillights pulsing like hot coals. I could still hear the muted radio and horn. A glorious interment, Roland. And then the lights were abruptly extinguished, it was silent, and air bubbles boiled over the water surface.

I turned and began jogging toward home.

I'd kept Scheiss's revolver. It was an old .38 snubnose with a cracked grip and much of the blueing worn away. There were five cartridges in the cylinder. The gun was risky to have around; no doubt it was registered to Scheiss and connected me to the murdered man. I didn't want it for self-defense or because I might have to eventually eliminate another "problem"—there would be no more murders. No, the gun and one of the bullets were intended for me if my great improvised adventure blew up. A few ounces of lead in my temple would avert the escalating horror of police interrogation, trial, sentencing, imprisonment. . . . I could spare myself that ritual public humiliation and spare Claudia and Dante and others a prolonged misery. One bullet and all of us were free. At the same time, I didn't *expect* to kill myself. My chances of getting away with the seizure of John Dempsey's family and fortune—his life—were fairly good. All I needed was a little luck. It was just that the gun was a way of hedging my bet.

TWENTY-THREE

Powdery snow blew obliquely across the road. There was very little traffic. The dashboard clock read 10:40. It seemed later, of course, very much later—murder takes place in a zone outside "real time."

The town at the east end of the lake was quiet for a Saturday night. The bars were still open. A few cars and pickup trucks were angle-parked along the curbs; a police car waited for the traffic light to change. The movie theater let out as I passed, and I saw a dozen people emerge into the light and cold, all of them looking stunned, disoriented, and breathing big clouds of vapor.

The Lakeside Motel was located on a strip that contained fast-food restaurants and used-car dealerships and souvenir shops, all dark now, and small, old motels. The Lakeside Motel was five blocks from the lake. It was a U-shaped complex with a miniature golf course on one side and a convenience store on the other. There were just a few cars parked in front of the units.

I stopped in front of number eighteen, turned off the car lights and engine, got out, slammed the door—motel guests arrive and depart rudely—unlocked and pushed open the door, flicked on the lights, and stepped inside.

The room was overheated and stuffy. There were two beds, a desk and chair, lamp tables, a dresser bureau, a dinette set, and a small closet that smelled unpleasantly of Roland Scheiss. On the walls were a couple of prints of sailboats, a wooden crucifix, and a sign that proclaimed: OUR GUESTS ARE THE FINEST PEOPLE IN THE WORLD and, next to the door, a notice giving the check-out time and warning larcenous guests that they might be prosecuted for the commission of the below-listed crimes and misdemeanors.

The place was clean, though not neat. Scheiss's things were scattered around: socks on the floor; a flannel shirt hung on a wall light fixture; portable typewriter; two cardboard boxes, one holding manila file folders and the other cassette tapes; a leather satchel of photographic equipment; a half-eaten Big Mac; empty bags of pork rinds and corn curls; an ice bucket half filled with melt water; an unopened bottle of rye whiskey. I unwrapped the celophane from a glass and poured a drink.

The pipes pounded as someone in another unit drew water. This room periodically shuddered in the gusts of wind, and a tree branch clawed the roof.

I skimmed through some of the papers. Poor old Roland. He was like a kid in certain ways, a cruel, devious, unpopular boy. The ugly outsider, neighborhood spy. He referred to this motel room as his "op center." Claudia was the "Female Subject," and I, of course, was the "Male Subject." Dempsey was the "Decedent." Roland's grammar and syntax were clumsy, and he never spelled a word the same way twice. The style was a fusion of dumb cop and dumb lawyer prose, naive and comical in its pretensions. Without his cunning and brutality Scheiss was just another yearning simpleton. Viciousness made him significant.

I packed everything and removed it to my car in two trips, then returned, wiped the surfaces I had touched, switched off the light and left.

Roland Scheiss has checked out. Left no forwarding address.

Back at the boathouse I spread Scheiss's investigative data—files, developed photos, tapes, transcripts, etc.—over the floor and systematically went through all of it.

Scheiss certainly must have been disappointed in the tapes. He had placed his sound-activated bugs in Claudia's bedroom and the adjoining sitting room. It was bland stuff. Nothing at all prurient here, Roland, no heated coupling of murderers, no wanton moans and cries, no inculpatory statements—no confessions, Roland. Just music, generally Italian opera; the opening and closing of doors; Claudia speaking with Dante or Mary; the television; Claudia humming or lightly singing a few phrases of some opera and once, for almost half an hour, her soft, sorrowful weeping.

There were fuzzy long-lense photographs (taken through the fishing shack's windows) of me and Claudia (usually with Dante nearby) standing on the boathouse deck or snowy lawn or walking on the frozen lake, talking and gesturing, smiling—none of the pictures revealing more than simple affection. Sorry, Roland, nothing there either.

Despite the evidence of the tapes and photos, Scheiss persisted in believing that Claudia and I were longtime lovers and had conspired to murder John Dempsey. His notes and documents indicated that he'd been unable to surrender that stupid theory. The actual evidence against me had been distorted by his determination to implicate Claudia. How could he have possibly believed her guilty of that crime, any crime? Couldn't he see what kind of person she was? *Your own foulness, Roland, impelled you to suspect an equal foulness in everyone.* Claudia's decency, her *innocence,* was a provocation.

But Scheiss was half-right: he'd been pig-certain that I had killed Dempsey, and he'd been halfway toward proving it when I'd cracked his skull with the tire iron. Circumstantial evidence, not enough to establish my guilt, but possibly sufficient to arouse the interest of a district attorney. The premise was false, the leaps in logic absurd, his case a matter of half-truths and wild conjecture.

There was not enough factual evidence at this point of his investigation to do much more than cause a scandal or provide the basis for an extortion attempt. My alibi remained sound. No motive could be established because the motive had come *after* what was actually a senseless, freakishly random murder. Even so, Roland was dangerous; he had to die.

It was possible, of course, that copies of some of these materials were stored at his Chicago office. And it was likely that he had confided his bizarre theory to Dempsey's parents in order to justify his fees. I couldn't worry about that now.

The frosted window began to glow with sunlight. I fried two eggs with bacon and made a brandy-laced cup of coffee.

There were so many details, loose ends, so many things that I must do and so many that I'd failed to do. It was all very messy. Each killing gave birth to a hundred lies, and each lie bred more lies—I felt surrounded by lies, immersed in lies; lies were the medium in which I existed. Reality retreated and all of the lies coalesced into an elaborate construction that feebly imitated reality. I could not always be sure now what was true and what false. Truth and lie seemed to possess an equal weight and force.

As for the consequences, I really did not care much. This was all a fine high-stakes adventure, with much to gain and everything to lose, and luck the determining factor.

TWENTY-FOUR

On Monday two investigators from the Sheriff's Department came to the boathouse. Both were young, under thirty, reserved but more polite—nearly deferential—than you expect of police. They stamped the snow off their shoes on the deck, wiped them on the inside mat, and then stood hesitantly, looking at me.

"Don't worry about the floor," I said. "I'll just swipe it a couple of times with a mop."

They shuffled into the room.

"I've got a pot of coffee brewing," I said. "Care for a cup?"

They removed their hats and opened their coats. The bearded man who had introduced himself as Detective Carl Olsen sat on the half-sofa; the other, Officer Henke, sat at my desk beneath a front window.

I went into the kitchenette and poured three cups of coffee. "Cream?" I asked. "Sugar?"

"Black for me," Olsen said.

"Just a little milk will be fine," Henke said.

I brought them their coffee and sat on a stool at the counter separating the living room from the little kitchen. Both men were red-faced from the cold, and Olsen had bits of ice in his beard.

"I've got some donuts," I said.

"No, thanks. No, this is fine. Thanks."

"Christ, it's cold. I can hardly keep this place warm."

"Colder than cold," Olsen said. "It's *cold.*"

"Twenty-two below zero at my place this morning," Henke said.

I lit a cigarette and said, "Smoke if you want to."

Olsen dug into a pocket and held up his pipe (I nodded), and we waited while he filled the bowl with tobacco, tamped it down, struck a match, and exhaled clouds of smoke that smelled like licorice.

Outside, it was a clear, bright day, dazzling, but dim here in the room. All of the windows were thickly frosted, and the light filtering through suffused the room with a sort of wintry twilight. Blue tobacco smoke formed into glowing nebulae.

"We're investigating the disappearance of a man named Roland Scheiss. You know Mr. Scheiss, don't you?"

"Yes."

Henke had opened a notebook on the desk and was poised over it.

"When did you last see Mr. Scheiss?" Olsen asked.

"On Thanksgiving, at a small dinner party given by Mrs. Dempsey."

"Who else attended this dinner party?"

I gave him the names.

"Do you know where Mr. Scheiss lived?"

"Chicago."

"Do you know if he rented a place around here?"

"Not that I know of, no."

"Did you know that Mr. Scheiss was investigating the murder of John Dempsey?"

"Yes."

"Mrs. Dempsey reported seeing car lights out on the ice late Saturday night. Almost directly in front of the house. Did you see lights?"

"No."

"Hear a car engine?"

"No. But it was blowing like hell Saturday night."

"But there were no car lights?"

Both men looked up at the big circular front windows.

"I draw the curtains after dark."

"We've had other reports," Olsen said. "It's pretty certain there was a car out there last Saturday night." He plucked some melting ice nuggets from his beard and placed them in an ash-tray.

"Do you think it was Scheiss's car on the ice?" I asked.

"It's possible. Can you think of any reason why Mr. Scheiss would be driving his car on the lake in front of this property?"

"No. It seems a stupid thing to do."

Henke looked up from his notebook. "Every year," he said, "assholes go through the ice or drive into open water. Cars, snowmobiles, iceboats . . ."

"Would you like more coffee?" I asked.

Both declined.

"Is Mr. Scheiss a friend of yours?" Olsen asked me.

"No."

"Just an acquaintance?"

"Yes."

"Did you get along?"

"Roland Scheiss is a disgusting pig."

Henke quickly glanced over at me.

Olsen appeared offended. "He is a lawyer, you know, and a former policeman."

"A crooked lawyer, a crooked cop, a crazy pig. Look, we don't have to keep fencing, do we? Scheiss is working for John Dempsey's mother and father. You've talked to them. They're probably the ones who reported Scheiss missing. Dempsey left a lot of money and property, and they want to take it away from the widow. The estate and the child. The only way they can do that is to savage the character and reputation of Claudia Dempsey." I paused. "Am I going too fast for you?"

Henke kept writing for a time and then glanced sideways at me, smiling a little.

"Scheiss was trying to implicate Mrs. Dempsey in her husband's murder. I was the killer, you see, and she was my inspiration. But you've heard all this, haven't you, from Mr. and Mrs. Dempsey."

"We're only doing our job, Mr. Neville."

"Of course you are. I'll help you. Scheiss knew the whole melodramatic murder plot was crazy, but he was milking the Dempseys for all he could. Fees, expenses, additional fees. He was trying to dig out something, anything at all, that would make Claudia look bad to her in-laws. He spied on her, on me, looking for anything that might convince the Dempseys to keep paying. Am I going too fast?"

Henke shook his head and continued writing.

"You say that there was a car here on Saturday night. Okay. You say that Roland Scheiss has vanished? Very well, he might have been out there Saturday night, prowling around, spying, most likely drunk—Roland was an alchy—and he drove over a weak spot on the ice or drove into a seam. That sounds *reasonably* plausible, doesn't it, gentlemen? More plausible than a bizarre murder plot."

"We aren't accusing you of anything."

"Not overtly, no. But you *are* investigating slanders. You think there may be truth in those slanders. You *hope* that the Dempseys' slanders are all true—that would make a big, big case; you'd be in the newspapers, on TV; maybe there'd be a book, a movie. Rich and famous Hollywood executive murdered by his very beautiful Italian wife and her playwright lover; family lawyer missing and believed slain by the deadly duo. You boys and the sheriff and the DA are salivating."

Olsen was angry. "We are merely investigating the disappearance of Mr. Scheiss."

"Sure. You do that all the time, don't you? Investigate the disappearance of a man who's been 'missing'—put that missing in quotes, Henke—missing for what? Thirty-six hours, forty hours? You don't say to yourself, 'Well, the son of a bitch *is* an unmarried adult, and it isn't terribly unusual for an adult male to be out of touch for a couple of days, on a weekend.' No. This is bullshit. Mr. and Mrs. Dempsey gave you some poison to drink, and you love the taste."

Both men were angry now but doubtful as well. They were small-town, small-time cops without much training or experience. Roland Scheiss, in his time as a Chicago homicide cop, had no doubt investigated more murders in a month than these men would during their entire careers.

"Just a few more questions," Olsen said.

"No. No more questions." I stood up.

Out on the deck, I said, "Claudia Dempsey has considerable resources. I'm going to advise her to hire the smartest, coldest, meanest lawyer around."

"I told you, Mrs. Dempsey is not under suspicion."

"Oh, the lawyer won't be hired to refute this murder horseshit. That's too absurd to bother about. He'll be interested in rumors, gossip, innuendo, cute leaks to the media. That kind of thing. He'll be watching for slander and libel. He will protect Claudia Dempsey's reputation the way a wolverine protects her young. Is that clear? Fuck around with Claudia Dempsey's reputation, and my reputation, and you two and the sheriff and the DA will all be back on the farm."

Ten minutes after they left I cranked open a window to vent the smoke and went out onto the deck. It was still very cold. Sunlight reflecting off the snow and ice hurt my eyes. The sun fizzed in a sky that was closer to apple-green than blue. A hundred yards down the shore some kids were skating and their blades made ripping sounds on the gray-black ice.

I was about to go back inside when I saw Claudia walking along the shore path. She wore a tasseled stocking cap, boots, and a bulky down jacket and matching red wind pants. At this distance and perspective she looked small, solemn, like a child in her snowsuit, and like a child she wiped her runny nose with a mitten as she came up the steps. Her face was pink from the cold, her mouth as red as if lipsticked, and her eyes—the pupils black pinpoints in the brightness—glistened wetly.

"You haven't a coat," she said. "You'll freeze."

"I was desmoking the place."

She followed me inside and watched as I closed the window and carried the coffee cups into the kitchen.

"Did they come to see you?"

"Yes. Would you like coffee? A donut?"

"No. What do they want, Andrew? I don't understand."

"Did they ask you a lot of questions?"

"So many questions! About Roland Scheiss and John and you. Roland Scheiss is missing."

"So they say. Did you see car lights out on the ice Saturday night?"

"I did see lights, yes. But that was all. It was very dark and awful out. What do these men really want? Please tell me."

"Take off your jacket, Claudia, while I make us cups of hot chocolate. Sit down. I didn't want to discuss this rotten business with you, but now I must. I'm sorry. It's stupid and ugly, really vicious."

"Is it about John? They are policemen. Andrew, is it about John?"

Claudia removed her woolen stocking hat, and her hair, charged with static electricity, stiffened for an instant, and I saw greenish sparks and heard a faint crackling.

She saw my look and smiled. "I am full of electricity in cold, dry weather. I shock Dante when I touch him."

We sat side by side on the sofa. Claudia looked at me with an almost-piteous fear and trust. She did not touch her cup of hot chocolate.

"Claudia, as you know, Roland Scheiss was hired by John's parents for the purpose of breaking the will, seizing possession of the estate and of Dante. You knew that, but maybe not as harshly as I've stated now. Roland Scheiss is—was, perhaps—a bad man. A crooked cop, a dishonest lawyer, a vile man in every respect.

"His angle—this is insane—his angle is that we, you and I, were lovers and that together we plotted and carried out John's murder."

"What? What? My God!"

"I don't know if Scheiss actually believed this nonsense or whether he was simply using it to siphon money out of the Dempseys. He might have believed it partly or wholly—he had that kind of mind."

"Evil. This is evil."

"Apparently he's been trying to fabricate evidence that implicates you and me in John's murder. Enough to at least arouse suspicion, incite gossip. A cop, a lawyer, would know how to do that. And he's been spying on us for some time, hoping to prove that we sleep together now and have been lovers in the past. Now all of this is ludicrous, we both know that, but remember that his purpose—the purpose of John's mother and father—is to attack the will by whatever means expedient. First, they want to delay probate. Second, to invalidate the will by demonstrating that you are a beneficiary through the comission of a crime. Third, they hope to have a court determine that you are an unfit mother. If then Dante is declared the beneficiary of John's estate and his grandparents are appointed executors of the will and guardians of Dante . . ."

We sat together on the small sofa, our hips and thighs touching, our faces close—faces arranged as if prefatory to a kiss. Her eyes were wide, dark, moistly glistening in the dim light.

"Do you understand all of this?"

"Oh, I understand, all right. I understand very well."

She was angry. Good. She was not weak and weary and timid anymore; she was angry.

"There's more," I said.

"Tell it to me."

"Scheiss was working another angle at the same time. He was taking money from the Dempseys, but probably not a substantial amount, and it wouldn't continue for much longer—they can't afford his fees and expenses. And so he came to me. He tried to blackmail me, us, by saying that he would turn over all of his manufactured evidence, drop the case, declare us innocent to the Dempseys, for a large sum of money. Ten thousand dollars in what he called 'good-faith' money, and more, a lot more, when the estate was settled."

"Then he did believe that we killed John?"

"Maybe. How can you tell with a man like Scheiss? Maybe he did believe it. But true or false, it didn't matter to him. The threat of filthy public lies can be as intimidating as the threatened disclosure of dirty truths. You don't have to be guilty of anything to be vulnerable to blackmail. Halfway plausible lies will do."

"Did you tell the police about this? The blackmail?"

"No."

"Good."

"But I told them about Scheiss's and the Dempseys' allegations, because they already knew of them."

"And did those policemen believe the lies?"

"They wanted to."

"Should I hire a criminal defense lawyer, Andrew?"

"Later, perhaps. Let's see how this develops."

"All right."

My threat to the cops of hiring a lawyer was pure bluff. A good lawyer would ask me too many questions, the right questions; I could not hope to fool an experienced interrogator.

"This is horrible," Claudia said. "It's madness. I want to go home. Just that. Home."

"Yes. Just ignore the lies and the malice for a while longer, and soon you'll go home to Italy."

"Oh yes! Please God, yes."

"The worst of it is probably over. I intimidated the cops, I think. They assume that Scheiss was driving his car on the ice Saturday night. If he really has vanished, it's logical to suppose that his car broke through. He's probably at the bottom of the lake at this moment."

"Good," she said in a hissing whisper. "I hope he's at the bottom of hell!"

"We won't permit this harm us, Claudia, or affect the way we think and feel and live. To hell with them. Let's go get Dante and take him ice-skating or sledding. We'll have a good lunch. We'll go out and have fun."

"Yes," she whispered fiercely.

PART III

Split Image

TWENTY-FIVE

There was a sort of winter carnival at the village on the west end of the lake, with ice-skating races, fishing contests, an iceboat regatta, and other events. The winds of the last few days had blown most of the snow off the ice. The day was cold but clear and bright, dazzling. Hundreds of people milled along the shore and out on the lake. It looked chaotic, riotous, a confusion of skaters, walkers, psychotic dogs, snowmobilers, fishermen, and, farther out, the swift passage of iceboats with their grating runners and snapping sails. One hundred yards offshore a slum of fishing shacks sprawled across the ice. Some people drove out in their cars and trucks.

I held Dante's left hand; Claudia, his right. The ice was gray-black and filled with webs of cracks and chains of elliptical bubbles. We could hear pings and rumbles from the water below, and the reverberation of new cracks forming, some sounding like fabric being ripped, others like the prolonged crack of a great tree splitting.

A few of the fishing huts were elaborate, like small cottages, but most were just tarpaper shacks with plastic windows and sooty chimney pipes. We wandered around until I located Scheiss's "winter chalet." It had obviously been appropriated: greasy smoke uncoiled from the roof pipe, and a MEN ONLY sign had been nailed to the door. I peered through the window; several old men were inside. One saw me and raised his beer can in greeting.

We walked farther out. Not every fisherman used a shack; some augered holes in the ice and fished with hand lines or flag sets. Fish, some still twitching, lay on the ice: perch, cisco, walleyed pike, and northern pike, one that must have been at least fifteen pounds. Dante would not move on until he was permitted to touch each fish with his forefinger. Several times, when he thought he wasn't being observed, he tasted the finger.

"God, Dante," Claudia said, "will you stop licking that fish slime?"

"A born sushi eater," I said.

We were cold, and Dante was tiring. I hoisted him up on my shoulders, and we returned to land. There were several bar-restaurants along the lakefront; I picked out one and we went inside and sat at a table next to the big window. I ordered a pizza, a pitcher of beer with two glasses, and a Coke.

"This is fun," Claudia said. Her cheeks were flushed and her eyes wet from the cold. "It's so good to have fun again. Can we go back out on the ice after we eat?"

"Sure," I said. "There are a lot of fish out there that Dante hasn't sampled."

"It's fun; it's fun. Thank you, Andrew."

That night, after putting Dante to bed, Claudia came to the boathouse for dinner. I'd bought a dozen perch from a fisherman this afternoon, and now I deep-fried them in beer batter while she sipped wine and watched me from a chair. With the fish we had hash brown potatoes, snow peas, a small salad, and a bottle of chardonnay. Claudia's appetite had returned. Usually she just pushed her food around on the plate and nibbled, but she had eaten four slices of pizza today, and tonight she was ravenous.

"No dessert," I told her.

"Okay. No room."

"Brandy?"

"Room for brandy."

I poured the brandy, added a couple of small logs to the fire, and hooked up my VCR to the television.

"I thought we might watch a movie," I said. "How about a Hitchcock? *Rear Window*?"

"Excellent. We'll watch *Rear Window*. Grace Kelly was so beautiful. When I was a girl I wanted to grow up to look exactly like her. I thought I could *will* myself to be Grace Kelly. But each morning when I looked in the mirror I was still Claudia."

We sat together on the sofa. Claudia yawned and took my hand. It was warm in the room and I thought about getting up to open the door for a moment, but I didn't want to break our handclasp.

No one believed James Stewart when he claimed that the man across the courtyard had killed his wife. The cop sneered. Thelma Ritter was skeptical. Even Grace didn't believe him at first.

Claudia had fallen asleep. She slumped against me. I studied the delicate curve of her eyelashes. I took pleasure in the smallness of her hand, its moist warmth. I inhaled the scent of her hair.

"Claudia," I said. "We'll see the movie another night. I'll walk you to the house."

She sleepily turned and embraced me. We embraced in silence, and then we stood up and she leaned against me, her eyes closed, while I began to undress her.

TWENTY-SIX

I finished the play in late February, printed half a dozen copies, and sent one to Laddy and one to Josh Silver at his California office. Laddy, enthusiastic, full of praise (". . . though of course it does need work"), asked me if he could show it to the people at the Zarathustra Theater Company in Chicago. They had a national reputation and had taken a number of productions to Broadway and off Broadway. I consented. A week later Josh phoned me from London; he had read the play and liked it very much (". . . though it seems to me that the third act is a little weak . . ."); however, he was tied up with film work for the next year. Would I consider permitting him to put on a West Coast production in eighteen months to two years? "Maybe," I said. Maybe. He said that his office would send me a contract to consider within a few weeks. Claudia told me that she loved the play; it was wonderful, so typical of me and, oddly—she could not explain it—reminiscent of John, too. She hesitantly asked me if I would dedicate it to the memory of John Dempsey. "Certainly, Claudia," I said. "That's what I'd intended to do all along."

People talk of a sense that informs them when an intruder has prowled their quarters. It is a near-mystical feeling that may not be corroborated by evidence. It might be a smell that lingers in the room; a vague sense that objects—the very air—has been disturbed; an inexplicable arousal of fear or anger; delicately nuanced perceptions that do not quite reach full consciousness.

It was like that the day after I finished the play. Someone had entered the coach house during the night. Who else but Frank Stoughton, the man with a thousand keys? I spent two hours carefully searching the place. Nothing of value was missing. Scheiss's revolver was still in its hiding place behind a wall panel in the storage room. The liquor bottles had not been disturbed. I could not prove it even to myself, but I knew that the son of a bitch had been here last night, sitting in the leather chair behind my desk, opening drawers and cabinets, prowling, touching, sniffing, savoring the sense of power one feels during such an invasion.

A few days later I saw the sheriff's investigators, Olsen and Henke, appear at Stoughton's place. They parked their car in the driveway, circled the house twice, and then mounted the porch steps. They seemed unaware that I was observing them from the gazebo forty yards away. I could hear them knocking on the door. They rapped lightly at first, then harder, and then one of the men began pounding with his fist. The door finally was opened, and they entered the house. I timed their visit: thirty-five minutes. No doubt they were still investigating the disappearance of Scheiss. But what could Stoughton tell them about that? Even if he had been spying on the night I'd killed Scheiss, had seen it all, the old man was more than half-mad, barely coherent—his testimony would not be believed.

The cops came down the porch steps, halted at the bottom while staring down at me. Henke lifted his hand in an abortive wave. I could tell that they were thinking about coming down to talk to me; but then at last they turned away and walked to their car.

You rarely saw Frank Stoughton during the daylight hours. He no longer worked, and so Claudia hired young Tom, my falconer partner, to attend to the yard tasks. Stoughton appeared only after sundown. You might see him at twilight, a cadaverous presence, lurking among the trees or slipping ghostlike from shadow to shadow. He lurked; he watched; he prowled. Late at night you might hear dogs barking or the startled honking of the geese that often gathered on the lawn, and you knew that Frank was out there somewhere, his slow, obsessive mind ticking over with thoughts that I could not imagine.

"You must get rid of the man," I told Claudia.

"I know. But it's so hard. He has no money, no pension, no people, no place . . ."

"He must collect Social Security money."

"A small amount, I think."

"Give him a small pension, then."

"I will, Andrew; I promise. When we—when I leave here. That won't be long. I think now he's really quite harmless."

I didn't believe that he was harmless. I worried most about Dante, so small and innocent and vulnerable, so tempting to the deranged mind. And Stoughton was seriously deranged. One windy night I accosted him beneath the big lakeside willow, and he responded incoherently, half-hostile, half-fearful, shaking his long bony head and clenching his bony fists, accusing and protesting unintelligibly in his gravelly old man's voice.

"Hello?"

"Hey, buddy, how're you doing? Miss your old pal? Worried you wouldn't hear from me again? Look, Andrew, you got to realize, I really am going to put you and the Italian bitch away for a long time. Think about that. Impulse murder. You kill a man face-to-back—may John Dempsey rest in peace."

The hair on my neck and arms stiffened when I first heard his voice, but there was an artificial tempo to his speech, with odd separations between certain words and phrases.

"Sneaky. I got a knife; he ain't looking. You know? He didn't expect your sudden frenzy. Dirty murdering shits named Andrew Neville and Claudia . . . insensate butchery. Guilty! Guilty! Guilty!"

I interrupted the voice. "Thanks," I said, "but I don't care to subscribe to any magazines right now."

"Guilty!"

I hung up the receiver.

Obviously Scheiss had taped our three telephone conversations and now someone—the Dempseys—had clumsily edited them into a jerky monologue. The Dempseys' stupid little trick was not itself a concern; what worried me was my initial reaction, a momentary conviction that this actually was Roland Scheiss on the telephone, with his caved-in skull and frozen eyes and smell of silt and seaweed.

One night I dreamed about the murder of John Dempsey. I had never been able to recall those few minutes of fury and blood, which might partly explain why I had never felt even a twinge of guilt. The murder existed as a fact, but not in memory.

In the dream I am high above the scene. Below me are the two men, a deer carcass and a steaming pile of entrails, bloody snow, and the big twisted oak. It is a crow's-eye view. I may be a crow in the dream. The details are vivid even though seen from a distance and at an acute angle. The men are foreshortened from my perspective. They talk, and soon they start shouting, but I can't understand the words. They are speaking an unknown tongue. They move about in little increments, shift positions slightly, adjust the spatial relationships between themselves and the other objects. The changing pattern of the two men, the tree, and the deer carcass is very complex and abstractly expresses the emotion implicit in the men's voices and seems also to prophesy what is soon to occur.

The juxtapositions change once again, and suddenly a knife—a shaft of light from my elevated position—rises and falls again and again. Blood sprays, freckles the snow; blood spurts. The knife continues stabbing and slashing until at last the air thickens with a damp red fog and my view is obscured.

TWENTY-SEVEN

Late on a windy Monday morning, the first day of April, Roland Scheiss—encased in a chunk of gray-green ice—lazily floated toward shore, toward the little beach in front of the house. My mind produced a mocking aural hallucination: Roland's voice saying, "Happy April Fool's Day, buddy."

Claudia and Dante were in town. The lakeshore was deserted now, but another sunny day was forecast and there would be people about later in the day: snoopy old Stoughton, workmen putting in piers, people walking or bicycling the shore path. . . . And there was Roland, a hundred yards offshore, indolently voyaging toward me in his craft of ice.

The lake ice had commenced breaking up several days before; he was entombed in just one of the many floating slabs. In a vague way I had expected his return, though not in physical form, not like this. I'd supposed that he might join Dempsey in a sort of psychic visitation; that is, I would eventually incorporate certain aspects of Scheiss (vile thought) into my mind. But this astonishing reappearance, on April Fool's Day, seemed more than merely bad luck—it was a function of nemesis.

I had been sitting out on the deck, drinking coffee and idly scanning ice floes with my binoculars, when I glimpsed one that, while not particularly large, was oddly shaped. It was thick and lumpy, with dim blurs of color showing through: a distorted patch of dark blue, a smear of yellow. The chunk of ice, because of its irregular shape, rolled clumsily in the chop. I could not actually see the definition of his body encapsulated within the opaque ice, but I knew it was there. Roland had been wearing a blue jumpsuit with a long yellow muffler looped around his neck on the night I had killed him.

I went inside, refilled my coffee mug, fried up some eggs and bacon, made toast, and returned to the deck. It was impossible to figure out logically; one could only guess. Maybe Scheiss had not been quite so badly injured as I'd assumed, and he had somehow managed to escape the sinking car and rise to the surface. He would not last long in that freezing water, though probably long enough to grab the shelf of ice or a fractured slab. His hands and clothing would quickly freeze to the ice. Scheiss would lose consciousness (if his smashed brain were capable of such a thing), die, but not sink into the depths. Then gradually, his body serving as nucleus, ice would form in layer after layer (in the same way a grain of sand in an oyster is layered around with pearl substance) until he became completely entombed.

Windy and unseasonably warm weather had broken the thick sheet of lake ice into variously sized slabs that, in just a few days, had melted to less than half of their original bulk. The lake was now about two-thirds blue water. And here was Roland, his icy shroud shrinking, being borne to me by the currents and prevailing wind. *Did you miss me, pal?*

I ate all of the food, finished my coffee with a cigarette, and again lifted the binoculars. It certainly was not obvious. Very faint blue and yellow blurs, a suggestive dark form within the gray-black ice, an unusually shaped floe. I reminded myself that I had powerful binoculars and a special knowledge. And I reminded myself that the sun was warm, the ice chunk approaching shore, and in two or three hours even the least observant passerby might abruptly halt, disbelieve, begin to believe, and then start thinking about finding a telephone. I had time, though, a little time in which to plan and to act.

For days ice slabs had been washing ashore and had broken into drifts like shattered glass. Now I listened to the ice chips tinkle and chime as the waves came in. It was a lovely music, delicate and elegant, a kind of otherworld chiming symphony. The music seemed directly related to the sunlight that sparkled prismatically off the ice and the open patches of water.

I heard Claudia calling. "Andrew? Andrew? You won't believe . . ."

Slabs of ice, big and small, dipped and collided and slowly revolved as they drifted counterclockwise from the lake's center. Many escaped the current here and were carried farther east. But Roland would not attempt to evade this piece of property, elude me. Not Roland. *Don't be impatient, Andrew. I'm coming; I'm coming, pal.* Come on then, Scheiss. Come on.

"Andrew . . ."

Claudia and Dante appeared on the shore path below and to my left. Both were smiling, vital, beautiful. "Hi!" Dante cried, smiling giddily. "Hi!" Claudia wore a pearl-gray suit with black pumps and a cloche hat. She teetered a bit on the high heels. The boy was dressed in a blue sailor suit with white piping, buckle shoes, and a French-style sailor's hat with a forked ribbon. His short legs could hardly keep up with his torso; he seemed always on the verge of falling. They were living illustrations of the possibility of happiness. They were three-dimensional in a drab two-dimensional world.

"Oh, Andrew," Claudia said, coming up the steps. "Good news, wonderful news."

Below, Dante suddenly stopped, leaned over at the waist to pick up a stone, straightened, and then awkwardly threw it into the water. He bent for another.

"The real estate agent you found for me?" Claudia said. "He was at the market. We talked. Andrew, he thinks he has sold both properties here. *Both,* the house and the farm. Free!" She pirouetted, threw her purse on the table, and collapsed into a chair.

She tilted back her head and let her arms dangle. "The buyer wants them both. He knows this place. He's looked at the farm. He's a sort of real estate developer type." She leaned forward with her elbows on the table and gazed into my eyes. "Sold, probably, except for the haggling. What do you think?"

"Great," I said. "Terrific, Claudia."

"What is it you say? I'm going to shake the dust of this place off my heels."

"It's great news."

"The Malibu property can wait. I can sell that anytime. Free. I feel madly free. Oh, I know it isn't certain. But the real estate man was *very* confident."

She wore only a little makeup: some eyeliner and a gloss of almost-colorless lipstick. Her eyes glowed; they glowed. I knew that even now some Italian women put droplets of atropine (belladonna) in their eyes to make them glisten beautifully, and for an instant I wondered if Claudia had done that, but no, it was natural; it was Claudia now that she was happy.

Dante picked up another stone, tried to hurl it out into the lake, but it went awry and hit him on the top of his head. He stood motionlessly for a moment, outraged, then turned (I looked away) to see if his humiliation had been witnessed. No. It was not necessary to cry then.

"Now we must . . ." Claudia halted, suddenly self-conscious, took a cigarette from the package on the table, and waited for me to strike a match. She rarely smoked; this was a nervous gesture. She turned to look out at the lake and, too casually, said, "You told me that you liked Italy."

"Claudia, I love Italy. And you. And Dante. And there is no force in the world that can prevent me from following you."

She smiled. "I might encourage you to fly on the same airplane rather than abjectly following."

"When?"

"Soon. Let's go soon. We'll turn the whole complicated business over to the lawyers and the real estate man and the bank. May—the middle of May."

"Wonderful."

"Well," she said. She looked blankly at the cigarette burning between her index and second fingers, as if surprised to see it there, then tossed it over the railing.

Below, Dante saw the cigarette fall, stalked over and stamped it out with his heel, then turned and scowled up at us.

"I'm Catholic," Claudia said. "You know that. Not a good Catholic, oh no, a bad one, but even so . . ."

"I understand," I said. "Claudia, will you marry me? Please. I've been dying to ask you, but I didn't have the nerve. I was afraid you'd say no."

"I say yes!"

"Here or in Italy?"

"Home, in Siena. And we'll live in Florence. If that's all right with you."

"It's only perfect."

"You can write plays, and perhaps I'll do something in the theater."

"Yes."

"We'll live in Florence, on the river—I insist we have a view of the river. And we'll also buy an old stone house with some vineyards in the Tuscan hills, and we'll go there in the summers."

"We'll bottle our own wine."

"Yes, and press our own olive oil."

"Make our own butter and cheese."

"I'll have babies and get fat."

"Not too fat."

"Andrew, let's have a party here on a weekend in the middle of May. We'll invite our friends. It will be a sort of engagement party, but we won't *tell* anyone. It will be our secret. And the next day we'll fly off to Italy."

"Yes."

"And now—I have some very good champagne in the house. Shall we drink the wine and toast our future together?"

"Yes, yes, but later, Claudia, this evening. There's a lot I've got to do today. And it will be better to celebrate this evening."

"Yes, you are right. Tonight we will celebrate, consecrate, and consummate!"

Dante, stimulated by our laughter, ran up the steps and hurled himself onto my lap.

I drove to a Wal-Mart and purchased some of the things I'd need: a chainsaw; a plastic rainsuit, trousers and hooded jacket; rubber boots; goggles of the kind worn by motorcyclists; a box of latex gloves; a box of three dozen of the largest plastic trash bags they carried; a good two-key padlock; a spade and rake; and heavy pruning shears. The last three items were available on the property, but I thought it best to buy my own rather than borrow them from Stoughton.

The garage beneath the coach house had room to park four vehicles, plus a large section that had formerly served as a mechanic's bay. There were wooden workbenches, vices, lathes, a portable welding machine, jacks and hoists, and tools—those tools that Frank Stoughton had not appropriated for himself—slotted on wall brackets. Everything was old, oily, dusty, but efficiently arranged. Against the far wall was a steel bin full of discarded automobile parts: an engine block, cylinders, brake drums, gaskets, an entire axle, scrap iron, sooty slabs of machined steel. I picked out a dozen things that were small and yet heavy.

Claudia and Dante were in the house. I did not see Frank Stoughton, though he could very well be watching from a window. I was not much concerned with Frank anymore; he was obviously addled, incoherent. I loaded the scrap metal I had collected into my car and drove it as close to the icehouse as I could without tearing up the lawn.

The cubical, thickly insulated room had been closed all winter and smelled foul. Apparently some of the square cedar logs behind the lead sheathing were rotting. I would have to replace the overhead lightbulb with one of higher wattage. And I must shovel out the sawdust so the center drain would not clog.

I carried all of the scrap metal and my morning's purchases inside the icehouse and locked the door with my new padlock.

Back at the boathouse, I opened a can of beer and took it out onto the deck. It was very warm for early April. The wind had not changed direction, but it seemed to be blowing harder now, kicking up a greenish chop that caused the ice floes to rise and plunge wildly. The drifts of ice chips along shore clinked and chimed and clattered.

I scanned the lake with my binoculars, but I could not locate the distinctive ice chunk that contained Roland Scheiss. Panicky, I stood on the table and looked south, then north, and then again directly offshore. No. Gone. I thought, Jesus, he's going to ceremoniously arrive at someone's spring lawn party or beach volleyball game. *"Ain't you never seen a corpse before?"* Sneering Roland, as always uninvited and unwanted.

Had I imagined the whole thing? Had my mind deceived me once again? Yes, thank God, it had to be: Scheiss lay in one hundred and forty feet of water, enclosed in a steel automobile and not a carapace of ice.

But then I saw the ice chunk. I had miscalculated the force of the wind and current. It was coming ashore about thirty yards to my left. It advanced a little with each wave, retreated a little with the backwash. The ice was dark but still partially translucent; you could vaguely make out the contorted human form within. A few inches of the fringed yellow muffler was exposed. The ice chunk lifted, fell, and I could hear it scrape the gravel bottom.

TWENTY-EIGHT

The ice chunk was roughly the size of a compact car, with an uneven shelf of ice extending out all around. If symmetrical, it might have looked like one of those illustrations of a flying saucer. The ice was intricately marbled with cracks and milky streaks and clouds of tiny air bubbles like microcosmic galaxies. Rotten ice, gradually breaking up on the rocks as I watched. The friable slab would go first, fractured into smaller and smaller pieces as the capsule continued melting. The entire mass would be ground into a tinkling drift by midnight. Chip ice tonight, snow cone ice tomorrow morning, meltwater by afternoon.

I went inside, changed into swimming shorts, old sneakers, and a sweatshirt, and returned to the deck. There was no traffic along the path for a time, and then a pair of bicyclists came by, and ten minutes later a line of schoolchildren with an adult at the head and tail, wound along the curving shore path like a centipede. An elderly couple who appeared dressed for the golf course walked past. Then there was a lull for twenty minutes before a puffing jogger, eyes on the ground, emerged out of the trees to my right and later vanished around a curve to my left. All of them had passed within a few yards of the ice chunk that, like a frozen placenta, enclosed the fetal Roland Scheiss. What was screamingly obvious to me had been ignored by them. There were other ice slabs crashing on shore or, farther out, rocking heavily in the three-foot waves. People in general were not very observant.

Even so, it was a distinctively shaped mass of ice, and it did contain dull blurs of color and, if you paused to study it, the blurred form of a twisted body. Possibly the corpse was difficult to discern at a glance because it was so freakishly out of place, anomalous. We usually see only what we expect to see.

I was stalling. I was leaving it to luck. And all the while the ice was melting, chipping, fracturing on the rocks, preparing to spill its grim cargo.

The phone was ringing inside the boathouse. I went in and picked up the receiver.

"Andrew," Claudia said, "Laddy just phoned. He and a friend from some theater company are driving up today. They want to talk to you about your play. Isn't that exciting?"

"When do they expect to arrive?"

"Around five o'clock, Laddy said."

It was a little after three now.

"We'll feed them, of course," Claudia said. "I thought I would return to the market. Can you think of anything special I should buy?"

"Anything expensive will suit Laddy fine."

"I thought I might prepare a Tuscan feast."

"Check the bar and see if we have any cognac left."

"All right," she said. Then, "Isn't it wonderful? They're going to stage your play."

"That's far from certain."

"Oh, it's certain. How can they say no?"

"I can say no if the terms aren't right."

"Don't be silly. It will all work out beautifully. It's a very good play, and Laddy told me that a very good theater company is dying to put it on."

I carried the telephone to a window. Three women were passing. The deck blocked my view of their bodies, and I could only see the three severed heads floating by. They did not hesitate farther down the path, opposite the ice chunk.

"Andrew? Did you hear me?"

"I'm sorry—what?"

"If—I mean when—when your play is produced in Italy may I play the part of Marie? Would you permit that?"

"Of course. Though Marie isn't a very nice person."

"Ah no, but it's a wonderful part!"

"I'll see you a little later, Claudia. Pick up some more good wine."

"Excellent. And after they've gone we'll have a celebratory carnal episode?"

"Absolutely."

She laughed. "Very well. I'll chase them away early. Bye then, darling."

Below the deck was a storage area enclosed by lattice panels. A gate opened into a crawl space stuffed with bouys and anchor chains, coils of rope, foam seat cushions, fishing tackle, a dinghy with a cracked bow, boating paraphernalia. I dragged out a sturdy boat hook. It was made out of ash, eight feet long with a brass hook curved like a question mark. While I was cleaning away cobwebs and a tangle of fishing line, a pair of boys, identical twins, rode by on bicycles. They were absorbed by the music issuing from their Walkmans.

The water immediately numbed my legs, and bone-deep within the prickly numbness were the first twinges of the coming ache. It was difficult to breathe normally. I had to hurry. I did not worry about passersby now—success depended on luck once again—but I knew that I could not remain long in that water.

The big ice chunk was grounded on some rocks. I drove the end of the boat hook down at an angle of good leverage, waited for a wave to lift the ice mass, then pushed hard. It moved a foot or two. I did the same thing several times until the chunk was again floating. Then, despite its considerable weight, I was able to lever it slowly toward the east.

Almost directly in front of the big house, at the end of the sweep of lawn, was a great old weeping willow with gnarled roots and widely spread limbs. One big limb grew horizontally outward over the water. I thought I might be able to wedge the ice beneath that limb. Pier timbers were stacked on the lake side of the shore path to a height of six feet and a length of eighteen feet. They would block view of the ice (and of Roland Scheiss) if I could maneuver it the last thirty feet before my legs cramped, if I succeeded in wedging it beneath the limb.

A ragged yellow strip of Scheiss's muffler had been exposed by the melting of the ice capsule. Maybe his mother had knit that muffler for him. Even Roland had had a mother. His head, torso, and one arm were blurred but unmistakable. I could make out the circular glint of his Rolex and the tiny fire of his ruby ring. His face was a white blur cocked quizzically toward me. *What's happening, pal?* His lower abdomen and legs were still deeply buried in the ice.

It became increasingly difficult to control my own legs. They were numb from hip to foot, with a deep interior ache, and I had to consciously will them into position. The coldness seemed to be seeping upward into my chest, chilling my heart and lungs, freezing my spine.

The forward edge of the ice struck the tree limb. I pried it out into deeper water, and then, timing a wave, I levered it beneath the limb. The wood twisted, creaked, and the thin bark split along the grain. It might hold. It would hold there until the size of the ice mass was greatly reduced by melting.

Using the boat hook as support, I waded into shore, crawled up the embankment, and sat with my back against the stack of pier timbers. My legs were a bloodless white and hard and ice-cold to the touch. The central axis of pain spread outward into the numbness. My lower back, my kidneys, ached. Muscles in both thighs began to spasm. I had never felt such pain. The coldness was now perceived as extreme heat, burning. I might have cried out then, except I heard voices on the other side of the pier, a man and a woman discussing the reprehensible behavior of "Kenneth" as they passed.

After fifteen or twenty minutes I was able to rise and limp painfully to the boathouse. I showered for a long time in steamy hot water. The muscles in both thighs and my right calf were sore from cramping. It seemed that the entire tracery of nerves in my legs were on fire—burning filaments. But I was able to walk stiffly, and I was relieved to have Scheiss out of sight for at least a couple of hours.

TWENTY-NINE

For Laddy, apparently, fashion-spring had arrived: He wore a white linen suit with a taupe silk shirt and black string tie and woven leather shoes that looked like heeled sandals. His white Panama hat had been tossed onto a coffee table. He was languid today, and his grip was moist and soft—shaking hands with him was like grasping a squid.

"Why," he drawled, "are you walking like that?"

"I pulled a muscle," I said.

"Really?" he said archly. "Which muscle did you pull?"

With Laddy was a man around forty-five who was more casually dressed in jeans and corduroy sport jacket over a collarless shirt. He wore round wire-rimmed glasses, and his thin hair looked dusty. His name was Barry Widenfield.

"I liked your play," he said.

"Good. Thanks."

"I'm going to try to convince you that Zarathustra should introduce it to the public."

Widenfield had been one of the five founders of the Zarathustra Theater Company. They had started in an Old Town loft and now, fourteen years later, were building a multimillion-dollar theater complex in the Loop. They had a very good reputation. Some of their people had gone on to considerable success in New York and Hollywood.

"What a great room," Widenfield said now, glancing around

at the huge stone fireplace, the raftered ceiling, the organ on its elevated platform, and the ascending uneven row of shiny brass pipes—like panpipes for a giant. "You could put on plays in this room."

"It's been done," Laddy said. "I myself was a bit player in a drama starring one Roland Scheiss. Incidentally, Andrew, I saw in the newspaper that this Scheiss has vanished. Did you snuff the odious fellow?"

Claudia, bearing a tray of canapés, entered from the kitchen area. "We don't speak that name in this house," she said sternly. She had changed into a black cocktail dress. She was stunningly beautiful and outrageously happy, and Laddy turned to me with raised eyebrows and a cynical look.

"Where shall I put these?" Claudia asked.

"On a table in one of the bays," I said.

"I'll join you later," Claudia said. "Laddy—do you like osso buco?"

"I did, until he betrayed me with another."

I made three drinks and carried them into the left glassed-in oval bay. It was after five and the light had softened, erasing the metallic glaze of lake and sky. Earlier I had opened one of the windows, but now I closed it—the breeze off the lake was quite cool. Laddy and Widenfield nibbled at Claudia's canapés while I stood for a time, looking down toward the rectangular white stack of pier timbers and just beyond to the high branches of the willow. *Are you still there, Roland?* It was absurd, this effort to behave normally, entertaining visitors and preparing to discuss aspects of my dubious future. It was like finishing out a chess game when you know you are almost certain to lose.

"Laddy tells me," Barry Widenfield said, "that Josh Silver is also interested in your play."

"Yes. He won't be free for eighteen months to two years, but he said that he'd very much like to put the play on in California."

"Did he say where?"

"He mentioned the La Jolla Playhouse, the Pasadena Playhouse, and the Los Angeles Theater Company. He said his office was going to mail me a contract. I haven't received it yet."

"I'm sure you don't want to wait two years."

"No."

"What if we have a long run in Chicago, and then want to take your play to New York?"

"Yes, what if . . . ?"

"Well, what if your contract with Josh conflicted with our plans, our proposed contract?"

"I guess it's your job to sign me up first and best."

He nodded, crossed one leg over the other, and pulled at his upper lip a moment before saying, "You surely know, Mr. Neville, how expensive it is to put on a good—I mean really good—production these days. We lose money on more than half of our plays, and we're considered extraordinarily successful in today's theater. We expect to receive certain concessions from the playwright."

"We're talking concessions already?"

"For example, we generally ask for a percentage of the proceeds from other, subsequent productions of the play for a reasonable period."

"Uh-oh," I said. "Concessions, percentages, reasonable periods. I guess this is what they call negotiation. I'll pour three more drinks. Make that two drinks."

Laddy was dozing in his chair. Every now and then he lazily lifted a hand as if to brush away a fly, but there were no flies.

Claudia joined us. She listened to the conversation, her head tilted, occasionally glancing at me with a little smile, and then she rose and said, "Dinner will be ready in half an hour."

"All right," I said. "I'm going to show Barry and Laddy the coach house. We'll be back soon."

"Come on," I told Laddy, pushing his shoulder. "Get up, you lazy swine."

"Gads, sir," he said, and he sat erect and covered his face with his palms.

I led them around the garage and up the outside stairway to the coach house.

"Nice," Laddy said, and he sprawled out on the leather sofa. "Gads."

I got a copy of the play from my desk and gave it to Widenfield. "I've made some changes in the third act. Start about halfway through and read to the end. I want to know what you think. I'm going down for a minute to see if Claudia needs any help."

The sun was below the horizon now, but the sky was still bright and the few clouds glowed incandescent pinks and scarlets. It was cool. The wind had diminished at sunset and shifted toward the north. There might be a frost tonight. No one was walking or bicycling the shore path now, and I didn't see old Frank Stoughton. I hadn't seen him all day. His health was poor. Energy was required to prowl and snoop and steal.

The ice block had melted some more, and big fragments had broken away. Three fingers of Scheiss's left hand were exposed along with more of the yellow muffler and some damp strands of his hair. Most of his face was visible beneath a couple inches of ice. The lenselike distortion made his features look oblong, as in a funhouse's trick mirror. Or maybe his skull, fractured by the tire iron, had been further misshappen by the pressure of the expanding and contracting ice.

The chunk was still much too big to move, but the ice was honeycombed, rotten, and there were many deep fracture lines. I said, "You'll be coming out of your egg soon, Roland." *Can't be too soon to suit me, buddy.*

Claudia had worked hard on the dinner, and it was very good. We drank a lot of wine. Laddy had fully awakened and told droll stories that usually featured a misunderstanding of some sort; Barry Widenfield and Claudia learned that they knew some of the same theater and film people; I pretended to be a good listener, but my mind was outside with Scheiss.

Late in the meal I stood up and said that I was going for another bottle of wine.

It was night outside and chill. The lake exhaled a humid cold that smelled like milled steel. The ice chunk was breaking up quickly. Scheiss's head, left arm, and left shoulder were free now.

I returned to the house, opened a bottle of wine, and carried it into the dining room.

"Well, my dears," Laddy was saying, "the beast phoned me next day and complained bitterly that the Meissen he had *stolen* from *my* house was *cracked.*"

We went into the big room for coffee and brandy. Earlier I had prepared the hearth with newspaper and kindling; now I started a fire and gradually fed in sticks and then small logs until it was blazing.

Claudia had drunk too much wine; she was talkative and coquettish in an ironic way. Widenfield told me that he approved of the changes I'd made in the third act of the play, but in his opinion it still required some judicious deletions, surgery, more fat cut out; a "literary liposuction," he said. He was drunk. They all were. I should have been drunk, too, but I was not; fear kept me alert, tense, cunning. I poured more brandy into their glasses.

"I'll go outside and get more wood for the fire," I said.

The moon had not yet risen, but there was enough light to see by. The ice drifts softly whispered and chimed. I had left the boat hook on the gravelly beach. I removed my shoes, socks, and trousers, picked up the boat hook, and waded into the water. My legs immediately began aching. I fitted the end of the boat hook into a fissure in the ice and lifted; a large wedge splintered off with a sharp crack. The ice was fractured all the way through, and I was able to swiftly break away enough to expose the upper half of the corpse. His lower legs were still ice-sheathed. *Come along now, Roland.* I threw aside the boat hook, dragged Scheiss up onto the beach, rested for a time, and then struggled to lift him up the embankment.

A muscle in my right thigh began to spasm. I beat it with my fist until it was quiet and then vigorously rubbed my bare legs until circulation returned. *Keep going. Don't quit now. No rest for the wicked.* I tugged on my socks and shoes, stood, and pulled up my trousers. Scheiss had frozen in a near-fetal position, with his knees drawn up, right arm pressed against his abdomen and the left lifted in a sort of derisory salute. It was simplest to grasp his left wrist and drag him on his back around the pier stack to the lawn.

Scheiss had been a fairly heavy man, and the layers of water-soaked clothing and the chunk of ice that encased his legs made the corpse even heavier. It required all my strength to drag him up the lawn. I heard Claudia laughing as I passed close to the house. Strong with desperation, panicky, I dragged the corpse between the house and the garage and into the little woods containing the icehouse. I opened the padlock, dragged him inside, locked up, and returned to the house.

Laddy was in the middle of one of his elaborate stories. They were drunk and didn't notice my long absence or my damp, soiled trousers, my perspiration and deep breathing. Later, when the fire had burned down to a pile of glowing coals, Claudia turned to me and asked, "Where are the logs you went outside to collect?"

"Christ, I forgot. I'll get them now."

"Tie a string around your finger," Laddy said.

Laddy and Widenfield left at ten-thirty. I walked them to their car, and we chatted for a while about the play, the evening, a fine dinner, good talk, "You both must come into Chicago soon and meet some people, tour the theater facility, you know, phone us in a few days, good night, good night . . ."

Claudia was sleepy. "I drank too much," she said.

"We all did."

"I'll clean up in the morning."

"That's a good idea."

"Do you want to stay tonight? The girl is off, and of course I don't want to leave Dante alone here."

I smiled at her. "I'll wake you in the morning. I'll steal into the lady's bedchamber and awaken her with a kiss."

"More than that, I hope."

"Be sure to lock up."

"I will," she said. And then: "It was fun, wasn't it? Barry seems nice. Laddy is wicked but charming always. We're happy, aren't we, Andrew? We're happy and we're going to become happier and happier until we vanish—poof!—in a cloud of happy stardust."

THIRTY

I closed the heavy insulated door, secured the inside latch bar, and then replaced the 50-watt overhead bulb with one of 200 watts. The room was brightly lit now, a glowing cube. The last of the ice had melted, and the cadaver lay on its back like a broken insect in a puddle of water. You could tell by the angles that both legs had been fractured by the torquing of the lake ice.

I cut away his clothes with a knife and pruning shears: jumpsuit; sweater; two wool shirts; long underwear, top and bottom; the yellow muffler; and regular underwear. Patches of underclothing adhered to the body. It took more time to cut away his boots and two pairs of socks, and then Scheiss was naked and ridiculous. Silly, porky, contorted little man. His flesh was cold and stone-hard still and roughly textured. He looked like an ugly life-size sculpture: *Pigman with Broken Legs*. His skin had a faint amber hue mottled with brown and purplish patches. And the skin of his face looked shrunken, drawn taut over the facial bones, and I saw a glint of teeth, a glint of eye.

I dressed in the two-piece plastic rainsuit, pulled on another pair of latex gloves over the first pair, put on the goggles and tied a neckerchief over my nose and mouth, and yanked the chainsaw's starter cord. The noise was terrible in the confines of the little room. The air soon filled with exhaust smoke. I planned my dissection: the head first (eliminate that reproachful glance);

the arms below the shoulder joints; legs at the knees and again at the upper thighs. Eight pieces.

I was in the center of the room, directly beneath the bulb, and my crouching shadow was projected onto all four of the lead-sheathed walls. It was easy to continue after I'd cut off his head. Then an arm. The frozen flesh beneath the skin was dark red, maroon, but there was no bleeding. He had not thawed much. The chainsaw's blade slowed when it hit thick bone or the complicated mass of bone, cartilage, and tendon at the joints. It altered pitch depending on resistance. The saw whined and screamed and spewed exhaust fumes. It was like sawing through a knotty oak log, and particles of flesh, like tinted sawdust, sprayed out of the cut. I could not hear my voice in the demonic roar, but I chanted the appropriate words: "Grisly, hideous, macabre, horrible, atrocity . . ."

But there was something perversely comic about it, too, and several times I laughed even though sickened by the noise and fumes and the sight of all those grains of flesh floating and falling like pollen. It was the hilarity of nihilism.

I finished, switched off the chainsaw and overhead light, and went outside into the clean, cool night air. Exhaust smoke venting through the open doorway blew past in pale streamers. A light burned in the upstairs of Stoughton's house. Nothing moved except tree limbs and their shadows. I heard waves washing ashore, the chiming of the ice chip drifts, the tinkly running of the creek, and a hissing as a breeze moved through the tops of the oak and walnut trees. It was eleven-forty. Late, but not too late for Stoughton if he was in a prowling mood. There were periods when he kept the hours of a vampire.

Boat. Stupid! I had planned to either phone the storage company and have Dempsey's powerboat delivered or buy an aluminum skiff and outboard at the Wal-Mart, but I'd forgotten. Tomorrow.

Now. Now the body parts must be enclosed in doubled plastic trash bags, weighted with scrap iron, and tightly wound with twine. Bury them in the flower garden plot. Tomorrow night I would dig up the bags, load them into a boat, go out, and sink them in different areas of the lake. Scatter Roland: he would not reassemble; he would not return again. And sometime tomorrow I must run a garden hose into the icehouse and scrub the walls and floor, flush all the filth down the drain. Burn Scheiss's and my own soiled garments? No, stuff them into another trash bag and sink them. Attend to all the details. Remain cool; be precise; *think.*

It was not logical to expect that I would get away with this, yet I was confident. People got away with this sort of thing all the time. No doubt at this instant men were comitting murder and cutting up bodies and digging shallow graves. There were killers out there, mutilators, butchers, cannibals—my colleagues.

It was not a bright night; there was only a half moon, and ribbed clouds moving in from the northeast obscured it much of the time. The first eight or ten inches of garden soil were loose, but below that the earth was compacted and I had to stand on the spade to get a good bite. It was not possible to be silent. There was the scrape of the spade and a clicking when it struck a stone. The moonlight dimmed and brightened and dimmed again. I was a little giddy with the madness of what I had done and was now doing. This isn't me, not *me.* I did the necessary work, and at the same time I felt outside myself, apart, observing and wryly commenting on actions that seemed dredged up from old horror movies and forgotten nightmares. This can't be *me.* My mind was split in halves, and once, for an instant, I believed that I was digging up a corpse and not preparing to bury one. And I was not digging a single shallow grave, but half a dozen holes that would soon receive the dismembered corpse.

At last, sweaty and fatigued, I leaned on the spade shaft and looked around at the scattered holes and piles of excavated dirt.

Well done—for now. Tomorrow night I would have to dig up the body parts, load them into a boat, take them out, and sink them in deep water.

I returned to the icehouse and packed Roland's remains into trash bags weighted with scrap metal and tightly wound them with twine. The torso, an almost comical object when separated from its parts, in one bag; the head (surprisingly heavy) in another bag along with one arm; a bag for each thigh; and one more bag for the lower legs and the other arm. Five bags, plus a sixth for our clothing.

I carried the bags out to the garden patch in two trips, dropped them into the holes, and quickly—seized by anxiety now—shoveled in the loose dirt and tamped it down with the back of the spade.

I roughly raked over the ground, oblitterated my footprints, and smoothed the six little mounds. Here lies Roland G. Scheiss. And here and here and here.

Finally I locked the tools away in the icehouse and, wearier than I have ever been in my life, climbed the stairway to the coach house office. From its windows I could look down and out to the garden, the gazebo, the bridge over the creek, and up the stretch of lawn to Stoughton's house. The upstairs window was dark now. What did he do in there at night? I'd seen no books in the house, no television or radio, nothing to distract or entertain. Perhaps he spent the long night hours (when he wasn't on the prowl) fondling his eccentric collection of found and stolen objects. Perhaps he just sat in his underwear and listened to voices. Perhaps he stood at a dark window and curiously observed killers and grave diggers attending to their duties.

I poured a water glass half full of cognac and drank it with the first cigarette. My hands trembled from physical effort. My legs ached. I desperately needed sleep. Everything was so confused. Each of my actions seemed severed from every other action. There were sequential absurdities. It was all muddled, awry, false, but I was unable to determine what had gone wrong and how it could be corrected. My actions were flawed because I was flawed.

An hour later I was awakened by noises from outside, snarls, coughing sounds, and hisses like air being let out of a tire. My dreams had been fragmented and reflected tonight's events: images of amputated limbs, sheared bones, a chainsaw scream issuing from the twisted lips of a severed head.

Drunk from brandy and fatigue, stunned by my dreams, I got up from the sofa and staggered to a window. Cool air blew in through the screen. Below in the moonlit garden dark shapes sinuously moved. Demons, half a dozen of them, fighting over carrion that I had buried an hour before. Furry, masked little ghouls. Raccoons. No tipping over garbage cans tonight; no scavenging through the garbage. This was a feast of protein, the avid, pointy-toothed recycling of Roland.

I ran down the stairs and across the strip of lawn toward the garden. Evil little beasts. Furry devils. I waved my arms. I heard myself growling like a dog. The raccoons scattered but did not retreat far. They were very bold. They moved away, backs hunched, fur erect, hissing, and then returned. When I chased one, the others advanced. They had dug up and torn some of the plastic bags. An arm with a crooked elbow and the fingers of its hand splayed glowed with a sort of phosphorescence in the moonlight. I saw a gnawed calf. Nasty little ghouls with their masked eyes and ringed tails. Quarrelsome eaters of the dead.

They were aggressive. I had to watch them. I stuffed the body parts back into the two bags and carried them to the icehouse. When I returned with the spade they had dug up another of the bags and were fighting over the contents. Stinking furry hump-backed hissing goblins. They snarled and fought each other; they advanced toward me as if to attack, then turned away. I chased them, swinging the spade, then ran back to dig up another bag, chased them again. Foul ill-tempered grave robbers. At last, defeated, they slipped away and vanished into the deep shadows.

I locked the bags in the icehouse, then once again raked and smoothed the garden. It had been frantic: had we—demons and I—made as much noise as it seemed?

Back in the coach house I poured another brandy. I *had* to sleep. It wasn't over; there was still much to do tomorrow. And then suddenly, in my drunkenness and exhaustion, I was struck by a flash of lucidity. Why, for God's sake, had I cut Scheiss's corpse to pieces? Why had I rationally (I thought) purchased the chainsaw and other items with the intention of dismembering the body and then tonight, just as coolly, cut it apart? And why had I buried those parts in the garden? Why hadn't I simply left the body in the icehouse, entire, until I was able to take it out and sink it in the lake? The butchery was crazy. The temporary burial was crazy. It all could have been done so much more simply and safely. Christ, I could have stuffed the corpse in the trunk of my car and driven off to dump it in some remote field or woods.

I was insane. It was a revelation. I truly was mad. Until now I had never doubted my purpose and my actions, but there it was: I was crazy. It was a surprise and a wonder to accept that hard fact. I knew that I would have no difficulty scoring high on an IQ test; and with a little prudent deception I would fall within the "normal" range after a battery of psychological tests; and no judge or jury would find me innocent by reason of insanity. Nevertheless, I was mad. For the first time since killing John Dempsey I was able to objectively view my acts, regard them as if committed by another man, and there was only the one conclusion—I was criminally insane.

But, I thought, pouring another brandy, but see here, just because I am insane at this instant does not mean that I shall be insane next month or next year. Many recovered from mental illness. You were sick and then you became well. You were careful about your diet and you took long walks in the country and you were scrupulous about taking your medication and with the help of your lovely wife and sweet foster son you became healthy. Of course, I would have to remain crazy for a while longer; there was a job to be finished tomorrow and weeks during which I must remain madly cunning in order to avoid discovery and punishment, but soon, in Italy . . .

Oh yes, I would slowly recover my health in a new country with my new family and new life. I could do it. The disease was deep and insidious, but I knew that I could defeat it when we reached Italy. I would then experience remorse and guilt. I would suffer. I would suffer; I would atone; I would heal. It was important, though, to remain crazy for at least another six weeks.

I awakened abruptly at dawn. The watch and ring! I could not recall seeing Scheiss's Rolex and ruby ring when I had severed his limbs in the icehouse. He had been wearing them earlier; I had noticed them beneath the ice. But I had dragged him up the lawn by the left arm and wrist. You could pull off a watch easily enough that way and possibly a ring, too, if it didn't fit perfectly.

They were not in the icehouse. I did not see them in the patch of garden. I searched the lawn for an hour without finding either the watch or ring. Stoughton? No. I told myself, You must stop blaming the old man for everything that goes wrong.

THIRTY-ONE

We gave the party on the second Sunday in May. It rained in the morning, but by eleven, when the guests began arriving, the sun had come out and a gentle warm breeze was blowing from the northwest. The land had turned a lush green during the past ten days. Now the trees and grass gleamed wetly, the air was scented by lilacs, and the lake—a sort of chemical-blue today—shimmered with crescents of light. "A perfect day," Claudia said.

The caterers had scattered some picnic tables over the grounds and trailored in a big charcoal unit. They had set up a bar in the gazebo. Musicians had been hired. Yesterday I had erected a badminton net and laid out a croquet court. John Dempsey's cabin cruiser was tied to the end of the pier, and the boy, Tom, would take guests on rides out into the lake. It was all rather elaborate and expensive, but Claudia was determined to throw this "secret engagement" party.

Only a few persons had been told that we would soon be taking a trip to Europe; no one knew that we intended to marry there and make our home in Italy. "We'll write to our few good friends," Claudia said, "and not concern ourselves with the others." She took delight in the secrecy, relished imagining the surprise and dismay our elopement would cause. In part, we had planned our clandestine emigration to defeat the possibility that the Dempseys might file a court action and delay our departure through an injunction; but Claudia enjoyed the intrique mostly for its own sake.

We had tickets for a Tuesday flight to Rome. Claudia's personal possessions would be shipped later. The house and farm had been sold to the real estate investor, and the business was now in probate. All of the household furnishings and other properties—boats, automobiles, et cetera—had been turned over to an auction house. The way was clear. On Tuesday we would board an airplane and fly off to a new world, virtually a new dimension, to my way of thinking.

John Dempsey's "ghost" approved of the arrangements. He—this psychic squatter—continued to repproach me during my late-night half-dreams, but he was eager to leave, to share Claudia's and Dante's lives in Italy. Roland Scheiss, more recently murdered and so not yet so fully formed in my mind as John, sneered and whined and threatened. He said, *I don't like Italians.* He said, *You ain't gonna get away with it, pal.* Of course I knew it was all craziness during the daylight hours, but at night I believed in their spiritual existence and their power. I relied on Dempsey to control Scheiss.

Claudia had invited many people, some of them near-strangers: neighbor families; the priest and a few parishioners from her church; business acquaintances: her lawyer, the real estate agent, Mathews, the soon-to-be new owner of the house; the Italian consul and his wife; the Chapmans, the soap opera couple, who were preparing to move to Los Angeles; and Laddy, of course; and Barry Widenfield, who had brought along several of his theater associates; and others whom I knew vaguely or not at all.

There were a lot of children, mostly of the running and shrieking age. Dante, red-faced and exhilarated, ran and shrieked with the best of them.

I had sent out only two invitations: one to my sister and her family (she did not reply) and the other to Clark Wheeler Crabbe, who had been a close friend of my father's, the lawyer I had consulted after killing Dempsey.

He was the only man present who was not casually dressed; he wore a double-breasted wool suit that fit poorly because of his weight loss and a vest and tie. Clark clearly was dying. You could see the sickness in his slow, cautious movements, the pallor of his skin and his cyanotic lips, and the dull, inward-looking eyes. But he willed his voice to remain strong.

"I came out of curiosity," he said. "I'll stay awhile out of wonderment."

We were standing on the little arched masonry bridge. The clear brook water divided around a boulder and converged below in a carbonated spume. Now and then you could see the shadowy darting of a trout.

"It's warm," I said. "Do you want to give me your coat and vest? I'll take them into the house."

"It *is* warm," Clark said. "Hot, even. More like midsummer than spring. But even so, I am chilled."

It seemed to me that the "chilled" was intended to carry two meanings.

"A drink, then?"

"Perrier with a squeeze of lime. No, wait—bring me a double scotch. No ice, a splash of water."

I walked to the gazebo and got into line. The bartender was having trouble coping with the early rush of drinkers. Laddy was there.

"Who's the geezer?" he asked.

"A family friend."

"He looks like a lawyer."

"He is a lawyer."

Laddy laughed. "And a politician?"

"He used to be in politics."

"A judge?"

"For a few years."

Laddy laughed again, accepted two glasses from the bartender, and turned. "It's in the face. That sour expression of cynicism and greed not quite balanced by moral fervor."

"He's dying, Laddy."

"And who is not, my friend? Who is not?"

I got the scotch and a bottle of beer and carried them back to the bridge.

Clark said, "I was surprised when you introduced me to Mrs. Dempsey. I mean, I had expected something quite different."

"In what way?"

"She seems genuine. A lovely, natural, unaffected woman."

"That's right."

"Which only makes this strange affair even stranger."

"She doesn't know."

"I assumed as much. That acquits her. But you—it's horrible, Andrew, evil, by God, if that word still means anything."

"Depraved?"

"Depraved. Malignant."

"Insane, would you say, Clark?"

"What *is* insane is how closely you've come to resemble photographs I've seen of the man you murdered."

"And monstrous?" I asked.

He finished the drink and crumpled the paper cup in his fist. "Why did you invite me?"

"So that you could say those things, and I could hear them."

"Well, it's done. I'll be going now."

"Good-bye, then."

"Good-bye, Andrew. I would tell you that nihilism is always punished, but life has taught me otherwise. Sometimes it is rewarded."

"Yes," I said. "Like now."

Smoke from the charcoal fires thinned as it rose and formed delicate blue webs among the tree branches. Cooks had prepared the side dishes and were now beginning to lay entrées on the grill, steak and lobster for the adults, hamburgers and frankfurters for the kids. Small groups of people were scattered over the lawn and along the lakeshore. Others were playing badminton and croquet, wading in the cold water, relaxing on deck chairs, or chatting around a picnic table.

"I caught you," Claudia said, grasping my arm. "Isn't it a lovely party?"

"It is."

"But some are drinking too much. How will we get rid of them when the time comes?"

"We'll close the bar."

"I saw your friend, Mr. Crabbe, leaving."

"Yes. His health is poor."

"I'm sorry. I liked him."

"He liked you, too, Claudia."

"Did he? Good. Now I must run off and play hostess. Barry Widenfield is looking for you. I saw him—oh, somewhere!"

Widenfield was standing by the lake, smoking a pipe whose bowl looked like a lump of coal and watching two adolescent girls wade thigh-deep in the lake. The girls wore bikinis with the bottoms cut above the hipbones. They postured and jumped and squealed as each small wave reached them.

"Leering at the pubescent girls, Barry?" I asked him.

"Yes, but not lustfully. Look at how awkward and gangly they are, Neville. Silly, gauche, harebrained. And in just a couple of years they'll be hormonally balanced and extremely dangerous."

"Claudia said you were looking for me."

"I brought the contracts."

"Good."

"It's all as we agreed. I thought we'd open the play in mid-October. That's rushing it a little, but . . ."

"October is fine."

"You're going to Europe soon?"

"Yes."

"When are you returning?"

"I'm not sure."

"We'll need you by late summer to help select the cast, do any necessary rewriting, sit in on the rehearsals—you know the drill."

"Sure. Keep in touch. We can fly back when the time comes."

"Good," he said. *"Last Night at Marie's* is a damned fine play, Neville. I expect we'll both do very well out of it."

I left him with the wading girls, who were obviously both annoyed and flattered by his steady philosophical gaze.

Old Frank Stoughton had come down from his house and joined the food line. He wore a filthy T-shirt, gray work pants, lace-up boots, and a plaid peaked wool cap with the earflaps lowered. People, especially the children, watched him curiously. He shuffled forward. His shoulders were rounded and his head thrust out. His long jaw moved; he was either muttering to himself or prematurely chewing his food. Frank had come armed with his own plate—rather, he carried what looked like a big oval serving platter.

Claudia, in the gazebo, caught my eye, grinned, and shrugged. She still had not informed him that he must soon leave the caretaker's house, nor of her intention to give him a small pension.

Laddy slipped next to me. "That the old family retainer?" he asked, nodding toward Stoughton.

I said, "He was not always as you see him now. That man won a Nobel Prize in quantum mechanics in 1963."

"God bless the fellow."

"It's sad. He can't do numbers anymore."

Laddy laughed. "By the looks of him, he can't do soap and water, anymore, or his zipper."

Stoughton turned away from the servers and stalked up the lawn toward his house. He had gotten both steak and lobster tail, a mound of beans, potato salad, coleslaw, rolls, pie, and a pitcher of iced tea.

"Looks like he's preparing for a long seige," Laddy said.

"He probably is."

"This really is a nice party, Andrew, even though I'm not used to associating with so many straight, bourgeois types. And so what may I look forward to? What do you have planned for the third act, so to speak?"

"I thought that when the crowd thins out, I might fly my bird."

Laddy was quiet for a time, and then, smirking, he said, "I think you'd better let the crowd get very thin indeed before you fly your bird."

The three musicians had set up their microphones and amplifiers near the weed and bramble patch that had once been a flower garden. They were loud and bad.

"Dempsey used to talk about his bird," Laddy said. "Astarte. It's astonishing how much you look like Dempsey. You could be twins. Sometimes I look up, see you, and get a shock—'Why, there's John,' I say."

"John's dead."

"Alas."

The musicians quit at four. By five-thirty most of the guests were gone, and the caterers had cleaned the grounds and taken away their equipment. A dozen or so people remained: Laddy; Widenfield and the other theater people; the Italian consul and his wife; the Chapmans (who had absurdly tried to persuade Claudia to audition for a part in their soap opera); the man, Carter Mathews, who was buying the property, and his wife and two sons. Tom stayed to help me fly Astarte.

"Maybe this isn't a good idea," Tom told me when we entered the mews.

Astarte was more than usually nervous; she bowed and hissed aggressively when I approached. Her beak parted; her wings lifted.

"She's awful spooky today," Tom said.

"She'll be okay," I said, moving closer, whistling softly until the bird calmed a little and I was able to slip on the plumed hood.

"She might take off. She'll see a gull or duck and take off."

"This is the last time I'll fly her, Tom. Then she's yours. The other birds, too."

I pulled on the gauntlet, gathered Astarte's jesses, touched her breast feathers, and she stepped up onto my fist. Tom stuck some molted feathers into a bloody chunk of meat and tied that to one end of the twenty-foot-long rawhide line.

Chairs had been placed around the perimeter of a big open space on the lawn. A few applauded (Laddy whistled derisively) when I carried Astarte to the center of the ring. The two Mathews boys approached for a better look.

Astarte was calm now, hooded and balanced on my fist, knowing that she would eat soon. She was very hungry. I counted on her hunger to bring her down to the lure.

The sunlight was steeply angled now, and the trees cast long shadows over the lawn.

I removed Astarte's hood. She tensed for an instant; her talons gripped my fist more tightly; the irises of her eyes reacted to the light; and then she lifted away, jesses trailing and tiny bells tinkling as she climbed in a tight vertical helix. Soon she appeared as small as a sparrow in the cloud-flecked blue sky. Her wings beat hard as she began a wide circle. Halfway through the circle she veered away and vanished in the west.

"Aw, damn," Tom said. *"Damn!"*

And I heard Laddy reciting Yeats in rich theatrical tones: " 'Turning and turning in the widening gyre . . .' "

I willed the bird to return.

" 'The falcon cannot hear the falconer . . .' "

"Wait," Tom said. "I think I see her."

" 'Things fall apart; the centre cannot hold . . .' "

I saw her, too, now, flying hard toward the sky directly above us.

" 'Mere anarchy is loosed upon the world . . .' "

Tom moved away and began swinging the lure in a circle. Astarte saw it, flew downward, then folded her wings and plummeted like a rocket out of the sky. The rawhide line swished, and I imagined I could hear the low whistle of air rushing past the bird's feathers. I did hear the bells, and then she was close, still diving, and it looked as though she would surely smash into the earth, but she braked. It was beautiful. She braked with her wings and fanned tail feathers. She twisted, dipped, leveled. I thought she was going to follow the lure as usual, but she angled off, flew thirty or forty yards, and settled down in the weed-choked plot of garden.

Tom got there before me. He turned, and the expression on his face, in his eyes, told me everything. The others, walking across the lawn, saw and read the same look, and some quickened their paces and others slowed.

Astarte was mantling over Roland Scheiss's head. It was partly concealed by one wing and a tall spray of grass; the face was gnawed, blackened, rotted; the eyes were gone and the crooked teeth were exposed in a rictal grin—but I had no difficulty in recognizing Roland.

Hiya, pal!

I had failed to dig up his head and dispose of it with the rest of the body.

THIRTY-TWO

Now.

The windows are black now, it is night at last, and the crime lab people who were digging in the garden patch have gone, although the yellow crime scene tape composes a grid of dimly glowing horizontals in the darkness below. The men were not gone long when I thought I saw Frank Stoughton appear, an angular, stooped shadow that glided from bush to tree to gazebo. He moves gracefully for an arthritic old man, as if he were ice-skating. He has an affinity with the night. But you can never be absolutely certain that you have seen old Frank, that he really is out there. Once you know that a man regularly prowls the night-time landscape you have a tendency to see him here, there, everywhere. Stealthy men, prowlers, stalkers are multiplied in your mind. They divide and become powerful. Still, I do believe that I saw the old man a few minutes ago.

What struck me most was the silence. Claudia emitted a soft cry and turned away; one of the Mathews boys said, "Jeez!"; and Laddy—did he think it was a prank, a plaster Halloween head?—gave a barking laugh. Then it was silent. People began drifting away from the weedy rectangle with its centered falcon-and-head (like a comic-horror heraldic device).

Uniformed police arrived first, then the Sheriff's Department investigators, Olsen and Henke, and then a mobile crime laboratory van drove down the lawn. The lab personnel pulled sterile white coveralls on over their clothing. One of them said, "Get that bird out of there."

"I'll do it," Tom said.

I gave him the gauntlet and hood and watched as, crouching, he waded through the weeds and easily managed to capture Astarte.

Olsen and Henke separated and talked briefly with each of the guests. They wrote down names, addresses, and telephone numbers and advised everyone that they might leave now if they wished. None elected to stay. They approached Claudia and me and mumbled thank-yous, awkward good-byes.

The crime lab men placed Scheiss's head in a Styrofoam box shaped like an ice cooler and slid it into the back of the van, and then they commenced raking through the weeds and dirt for additional evidence. Uniformed cops strung up the crime scene tape.

Claudia came to me. She was shivering. She touched my arm. "I'm going into the house."

"I'll join you soon."

"Thank God Dante didn't see that. Thank God he was napping. Thank God."

One of the crime lab men found a half-buried patch of plastic trash bag.

"You'll be around tonight, won't you?" Olsen asked me.

"Yes," I said.

"And the lady?"

"She'll be here."

"See you, then," Henke said, and the two men walked to their car.

I thought about going to Claudia. She needed comforting. But not by me, not anymore, and so I turned and walked toward the coach house.

This morning I had everything; now I am left with only Scheiss's revolver—that cold, heavy little machine. It softly clicks three times when you cock the hammer. Soon I'll walk down to the lake and sit beneath the big weeping willow.

It is a beautiful spring night, clear and balmy, pollen-scented. There will be a nearly full moon later, but I won't wait for it to rise; the police will return soon with their warrants and accusations and handcuffs. No. I could face the police; I could face years in prison; I can face anything except Claudia's expression when she realizes the full extent of my treachery.

So, a few minutes to appreciate the night, and then. Oh yes, then . . . It must be performed coldly and consciously and with style. You lift the revolver and place the muzzle against your temple at the correct angle; you cock the hammer, listening to the three distinct clicks; you curl your finger around the trigger and, with less force than it takes to depress this computer key, you pull the trigger. Eternity.

Dempsey is here with me now, a comforting presence. Scheiss is here, too, sneering, mocking, vulgar. He is raucously pleased that I am using his gun to end my life. *But do you got the guts, Andrew?*

John Dempsey is sympathetic. *Andrew,* John says, *we all were going to Florence together, remember? We—you and me and Claudia and Dante—we were going to live in a crumbling old palazzo overlooking the river, with maybe a stone summer house in the Tuscan hills, where we'd make our own wine and cheese. Wait. Listen to me. Can't you wait? There is still a chance . . .*

I knew that both of them would accompany me down to the lake, sit with me beneath the willow, observe (one sad, the other triumphant) as I erased myself and those remnants of them that existed in my mind.

Well, then. No suicide note, or rather this long and elaborate note—if someone has the wit and skill to salvage my narrative from the computer.

Christ, stop stalling. I shall switch off this machine, pick up Scheiss's gun and the bottle of fine cognac, go outside, and get it done. Last words? Sure.

EXIT Neville

PART IV

RIP

THIRTY-THREE

Macabre Discovery during Mother's Day Picnic

Last night police arrested Frank B. Stoughton, 77, of 5978 South Lakeshore Drive, Lake Marquette, for the murders of playwright Andrew Neville, 44, also of Lake Marquette, and Roland G. Scheiss of Chicago. District Attorney Sheila N. McDonald states that she expects to file charges against Mr. Stoughton within the next few days.

The arrest was made in the aftermath of a grisly episode involving the discovery of the severed head of Mr. Scheiss on the lakeside estate of Mrs. Claudia Dempsey during a Mother's Day lawn party Sunday. A police spokesman reports that a falcon, owned and trained by Mr. Neville, found the decomposed head in an overgrown plot of garden.

Mr. Scheiss, a lawyer and former Chicago homicide detective, has been missing since early January. Sheriff Dalton Lindberg said that Mr. Stoughton has been the prime suspect in that disappearance, but charges were not filed because of insufficient evidence.

Sheriff's Department investigators Carl Olsen and Glenn Henke left the crime scene in charge of subordinates late Sunday afternoon in order to obtain search and arrest warrants from Judge George Patterson of Criminal Court, and when they returned that evening they found the body of Neville beneath a tree near the lakeshore. He had been shot once in the head with a weapon registered to Mr. Scheiss and found in the possession of Frank Stoughton during a search of the accused man's premises. Police report that they discovered a secret compartment in the house containing Scheiss's revolver, recently fired, and a watch and ring identified as belonging to Scheiss, as well as a great many other stolen objects. "It was a treasure trove," Detective Olsen told the Gazette.

A bottle of brandy and a half-smoked cigar were found with Neville's body. Police speculate that Neville may have been brooding on the shocking event of that day when Stoughton crept up behind him and fired one shot into his brain.

Stoughton, who was the caretaker of the estate owned by Mrs. Dempsey, was known to the police as a petty thief and Peeping Tom. In 1991 he served six months in the county jail after being captured while prowling a vacant house in the village of Clear Springs.

An official source reports that the mobile crime lab personnel, who conducted an exhaustive search of the property last night and today, found evidence that suggests that Stoughton killed Scheiss and dismembered the corpse in an unused icehouse on the property. So far only the head has been recovered.

Mr. Neville, who rented a converted boathouse on the Dempsey estate, was well known in Chicago theater circles for two plays produced in the eighties. Police refused to speculate on the motive for the murder of Scheiss but suggest that Stoughton may have feared that his neighbor had information connecting him to the Scheiss killing. "Neville paid for Frank's paranoia."

Mrs. Dempsey, who was briefly hospitalized after the discovery of Neville's body, was unavailable for comment. As Claudia Caporale, Mrs. Dempsey appeared in many movies in the U.S. and Europe. In a grim sidelight, Mrs. Dempsey's husband, John Dempsey, a well-known television writer and producer, was murdered last October while on a hunting trip to the northern part of the state. No arrests have been made in that homicide.

THIRTY-FOUR

**Triple Confession by Lake "Headhunter"
Police Ask: Are There Other Victims?**

Today District Attorney Sheila McDonald announced that Frank Stoughton, arrested Sunday for the murders of Andrew Neville and Roland G. Scheiss, has also confessed to killing the famous TV executive John Dempsey. Dempsey was brutally murdered last fall while on a hunting trip to Eagle's Nest in the northern part of the state.

While the DA declined to comment on the collateral evidence collected in the Dempsey case so far, stating she did not want to imperil the continuing investigation, she did say that Mr. Stoughton is unable to account for his whereabouts during the crucial time frame. "And," she told reporters, "Mr. Stoughton knows details of that crime that only the assailant would know."

She also said that, for the present, charges would not be filed against Stoughton for the Dempsey and Scheiss murders. "We're going to charge him for just the Neville murder now," she said. "At Stoughton's age, one life sentence ought to suffice."

Walter Schuetz, Stoughton's court-appointed attorney, said that his client was incapable of understanding the charges against him or intelligently participating in his defense. "He is insane," Schuetz said. "Insane according to the McNaughton Rule or any other rule, law, precedent, or variety of common sense."

Schuetz told the Gazette that he

intended to ask the court to have Stoughton subjected to psychiatric evaluation. "The man is clearly not legally responsible for his crimes," he said. "He belongs in a mental institution."

For more on the "Severed Head Picnic" turn to pages 5 and 6, this section.

THIRTY-FIVE

Andrew Neville, 44, Chicago Playwright

Andrew Neville, a dramatist whose plays were produced in Italy and Great Britain as well as the United States, died on May 19 at Lake Marquette, Wisconsin.

Mr. Neville, who was born in Chicago and resided there until autumn of last year, received a bachelor of arts degree from Northwestern University in 1974 and in 1979 and again in 1982 taught in Northwestern's Theater Arts Department.

In 1983 Mr. Neville's first play, *Let Them Dance,* was produced by the now-defunct Harlequinade theater group and, although not a commercial success, received many favorable reviews. His second play, *Payback,* was both a critical and commercial success, and saw production by many amateur and professional theater groups around the United States. It was also presented to audiences in London and Milan.

Mr. Neville's "long creative silence," according to his close friend and theater associate Aladdin Rawling, was to be broken by a new play, *Last Night at Marie's,* scheduled for production next October by the Zarathustra Theater Company of this city. *Marie's,* said Mr. Rawlin,"is surely the playwright's finest work." Production will proceed as planned.

Mrs. Claudia Dempsey, a friend of the decedent, announces that visitation will be from 9:00 a.m. to noon Thursday at the Sorrel Brothers Funeral Home, Clear Springs, Wisconsin. Mr. Neville will be interred in a plot adjoining that of his longtime friend, John Dempsey, at Foxhill Cemetery at 2:00 p.m. Thursday.